FI

D1587847

Winter's Crimes 4

WINTER'S CRIMES 4

Edited by George Hardinge

Macmillan

SBN: 333 13881 3

First published 1972 by
MACMILLAN LONDON LTD
London and Basingstoke
Associated companies in New York Toronto
Dublin Melbourne Johannesburg & Madras

Printed in Great Britain by
RICHARD CLAY (THE CHAUCER PRESS), LTD
Bungay, Suffolk

Contents

Editor's Note

In 1972 *Winter's Crimes* reaches the age of four years when its partner, *Winter's Tales*, becomes eighteen.

My task ends with thanking and congratulating the contributors – I have been lucky in the collection of such splendid stories by celebrated professional novelists – and in emphasising once more that:

None of these stories has previously been published – *all are new*.

GEORGE HARDINGE

SO MUCH LIKE ME

by George Baxt

I was kneeling on the kitchen floor with my head in the oven when the phone rang. Anyone with a stronger character than mine would have ignored the interruption and continued with this sorry business of self-destruction, especially as from the moment I had come to the decision to commit suicide, it had taken three days to select the method, muster the courage and finally spur myself into this ultimate action. I did my best to prove to myself I was made of sterner stuff, as I had proved to myself (much to my delight and surprise) on at least three previous occasions. So while the telephone continued nagging like some ubiquitous shrew, I inhaled deeply which brought on a coughing fit. I had heard of fits like these bringing on heart attacks or fatal haemorrhages which of course frightened the hell out of me, so I staggered to the sink for a glass of water.

Relief came almost instantly, but not from the telephone. It was still agonising away, which was a clue to the probable identity of the dauntless party at the other end. My money was on Maud Magruder. Maud was one of that peculiar breed of rich (she said), middle-aged American widows who chose to settle in London for the sole purpose, it seemed to me, of preying on unattached middle-aged men like myself.

I made my automatic move of reaching for cigarettes and lighter when I realised with horror and a cold shudder in this gas-filled room I might blow myself up. I turned off the five jets and then flung open the window and was immediately attacked by a hurricane of freezing wind. I drew my cardigan tightly around me for fear of pneumonia and rushed for the sitting room.

'Hello,' I said weakly into the mouthpiece.

'Oh, darling! You *are* at home! Did I get you out of the bath?' It was Maud Magruder.

'No, Maud, I was just lying down.'

'You're not ill or anything, are you?'

Her concern was as automatic and impersonal as the machinery making this connection.

'I'm not ill. I just don't feel very well.'

'You sound perfectly ghastly. How long have you been back?'

'Three days,' I said without thinking and found a renewed incentive to kill myself.

'Three *whole* days! And you didn't *call*?' I could see that indignant look on her face, the one she had mastered and reserved to fill you (especially me) with guilt. Where Medusa's look turned men to stone, Maud's turned me into jelly. ('Oh darling you didn't go see that movie without me. You *know* I was dying to see that movie!' 'You wretched scoundrel! You had an invitation to that opening and took someone *else*?' 'Blackguard! You know I've been *aching* to meet the Goshawks and you took Bernice *Grimshaw* to their cocktail party?')

I tempted the Fates and lied. 'I called you the day I got back but you weren't at home.'

'What day was this? Wednesday?'

'Wednesday.'

'What time did you call?'

'Oh, for Christ's sake, Maud, I don't remember what time I called.'

'I was home all day Wednesday.'

I stretched out on the couch and longed for a cold

towel to place across my forehead. 'I'm positive I called,' I continued lying brazenly, unconcerned at the consequence, knowing full well that soon I'd be back in the kitchen with my head in the oven, but this time with the phone off the hook.

'There's no need to sound so testy!'

I thought I had sounded bored. 'Let's not have an argument, Maud, I'm just not in the mood for an argument.'

'Then you really must be ill.' I wheezed into the mouthpiece but said nothing. 'Is that why you cut the trip short?'

'More or less.'

'Oh?' I could almost hear her cosying up to the phone. 'Is Kurt there with you?'

'No.'

'You didn't come back *alone*, did you?'

'I did.'

'Where did you leave *Kurt*?'

'Somewhere in Scotland.'

'Well I'll be damned.' Wishing won't make it so. 'How'd you get *back*?'

'I walked.'

'You *are* testy.'

'I took the train from Aberdeen.'

'Why didn't you fly?'

'I thought it might make me nauseous.'

'I just knew you two would have a fight somewhere along the way. You did *have* a fight, didn't you?'

I was positive I heard her licking her lips. Maud Magruder thrived on other people's disasters. Tell Maud Magruder a mutual friend has a terminal disease and she'll insist on picking up the cheque at dinner. Tell Maud mutual friends are divorcing and she'll announce a party catered by Fortnum and Mason. A really good day for Maud was when the *Herald-Tribune* obituaries listed a minimum of three of her contemporaries.

I must have lain silent for close to thirty seconds staring at the ceiling. Maud of course accepted the silence as a tacit corroboration. 'What did you fight about?'

'Everything.'

'Oh, come now!'

'He got on my nerves.'

'Well, of course he did,' she gurgled, 'you two are so alike!'

You've got to meet Kurt Bergmann. You'll adore him. He's so much like you.

'I'm sure you know I didn't like him from the moment you introduced us.' Maud's voice was unpleasantly shrill. 'Why does Bernice Grimshaw insist on thrusting so many unpleasant people upon you?'

I couldn't resist it. 'Bernice introduced *us*.' I heard her intake of breath followed by a brief pause and then an outburst of laughter. I can never win.

'Have you heard from Kurt?'

'No.'

'It's just as well.'

'I agree with you.'

'Oh, that must have been one lulu of a fight!'

'I prefer not to discuss it.'

'As you wish.' Her voice was stiff with starch. 'I don't suppose by any chance you're free tonight?'

I wanted to say, 'With any luck, I'll soon be free forever.' Instead I said, 'I told you I wasn't feeling very well.'

'It's just that I'm having a divine bunch in tonight for drinks and dinner. The Escuderos are bringing Tony Gompers.'

'Yes?'

'Tony *Gompers*. The *cellist*.'

'Never heard of him.'

'You must be going out of your mind! *You* took me to his recital last spring! How could you forget? You thought he was immensely gifted. You couldn't have forgotten. I remember saying at the time, coming from a brilliant musician like yourself that was *indeed* a compliment. I mean *you* who said Artur Rubenstein was an arthritic hack.' Another pause. 'You're pulling my leg.'

Fat chance. 'I'm sorry, Maud, I'm a bit vague today. Yes, I remember Tony Gompers, and he was good.'

'Well, his wife's just left him for a flautist, and the Escuderos are helping him get over her. Oh, do come! He's so terribly lonesome and the Escuderos say he does need a friend to talk to.'

'That's what Bernice said about Kurt when *he* left *his* wife.'

'Oh, to hell with Kurt!'

I silently agreed with her.

'Are you still there?'

'Yes, of course I am.' I made no attempt to disguise my rising irritation.

'Darling ... you're not in one of your ... *moods* again, are you?'

My moods are famous, perhaps more correctly in-famous. All great artists are prey to them. My moods are matched only by my monstrous temper. Perhaps you remember the headlines when I threw the piano stool at that deplorable conductor during my last public concert two years ago. I haven't performed in public since then. There were five months in that so-called rest home during which my solicitors effected an out-of-court settlement with that so-called conductor's widow.

Thanks to my so-called breakdown, I escaped prosecution. During the past year-and-a-half of my self-imposed retirement, I have attempted suicide (wittingly) on seven different occasions. The scars on my wrists are the results of four of those attempts. It was Maud who unkindly suggested I have my wrists fitted with zippers to minimise future efforts.

I really have nothing to live for. I have suffered three disastrous marriages and the notorious court case in which I sued my despicable parents for an accounting of my earnings as a child prodigy (I had mastered every Chopin prelude by the age of four, and at five stunned the musical world by playing *The Minute Waltz* in thirty-three seconds. I filled the time remaining with *The Happy Farmer*) left an ugly scar on my psyche. I received a very bad press when I refused to attend their joint funeral following the tragic car accident when I was driving them to Brighton during an attempted reconciliation. I had miraculously been thrown from the car before it went over the cliff. So I am very much alone in the world, without friends (Maud Magruder is hardly an incentive to go on living), unloved (my wives didn't marry me, they married my reputation) and my gift completely dissipated (the piano in my sound-proofed studio hasn't been tuned in over eighteen months).

'*Zoltan!*'

'What? What?' I stared at the phone and realised it was Maud who had shouted my name. 'Oh, Maud, I am sorry . . . I think I dozed off!'

'Well, thank you very much for *that*!'

'Don't be angry . . . you just don't understand . . .'

'Zoltan,' her voice was unusually soft and filled with understanding, 'you're crying.'

'No, I'm not,' I said between sniffles, 'I think I'm

catching a cold. The ... the window's open in the kitchen and I'm lying in a draught.'

'What shall we do with you?' I heard her tongue clucking. 'Now, darling, pull yourself together and come to dinner.'

'I really don't ...'

'I will not take no for an answer. Tony Gompers is just what you need. He's talented and witty and terribly attractive ... honestly, darling, he's so much like you.'

'Flatterer.'

'I'll expect you at seven. Meantime, sit in a hot tub.' She hung up before I could remonstrate and I slammed my phone down on the receiver. I stomped into the kitchen like a petulant child and tested the air there with a huge sniff. All trace of gas had disappeared. I banged the window shut and broke into a fit of sneezing. I left the kitchen and tramped with a house-shaking stride to my sound-proofed studio at the rear of my house. There was the piano in the middle of the room, untouched, unloved, unwanted like myself. I stifled a sob as my eyes moved around the room. The six lithographs I had always intended to hang on the walls were still stacked in a corner, on the floor the hammer and the tin of nails. The studio had been constructed by order of my solicitors during my stay in the rest home. The suggestion had been put to them by my psychiatrist. He, of course, had meant well. It would be there awaiting what he called 'my new beginning'. I didn't want a new beginning. I dismissed it along with my psychiatrist. I know my gift has also been my curse. Rejecting the piano was my way of exorcism.

Of course I attended Maud's dinner party. She's made of sterner stuff than I. I assure you, I'll be back at that oven again, but not to prepare a meal. Frankly, my curiosity overcame my will to die. I wanted to meet Tony Gompers. It fascinates me and piques my interest when someone says to me, 'You must meet so and so, he's so much like you.' It's what drew me to Bernice Grimshaw's that night six weeks ago when she tempted me with Kurt Bergmann. They say one should profit by one's mistakes, but I'm a different sort of speculator. I'm not particularly religious, but I felt Maud's phone call that afternoon had in some way been preordained. I was not meant to die then. I was meant to meet Tony Gompers.

If you're as myopic as I am, then you can honestly say Maud Magruder was a vision in her silver lame pants suit, silver-rimmed harlequin glasses that could have covered two faces instead of just hers and glittering sandals to cut down her height which was perhaps an inch short of six feet. Her face as always looked as though the cosmetics had been applied by an undertaker and very thoughtfully (some might say thoughtlessly) one of my recordings was permeating the room with a Brahms Piano Concerto from four cleverly concealed speakers.

Her left cheek brushed my right cheek as though I might carry an infection. 'How good of you to come, darling,' she said in her party voice which was terribly British except for the flat a's which were always a dead giveaway of her midwestern American origin. I greeted Alphonse and Lolita Escudero who were once successful ballroom dancers and now owned dancing schools in every European capital. They were immensely wealthy and collected musical celebrities and sometimes managed to trade them with friends who had collected a better musical celebrity than they had been able to acquire. There were others present of course, but they are not important to this story.

Maud took my hand and guided me to Tony Gompers who was leaning disconsolately against the grand piano, and although I knew better, I expected him at any moment to break into *Stout Hearted Men*. I had recognised him as we were crossing the room and passed Maud's dull-faced Spanish maid holding a tray of canapes in front of her as though to take one might tip the balance. It did my ego good when Tony brightened at the mention of my name and Maud beamed like a good deed in a naughty world.

'I just *know* you two have a great deal to talk about,' insisted Maud and she left us, to join her other guests at the opposite side of the cavernous room.

'Maud was afraid you might not come,' said Tony.

'Maud is never afraid,' I replied somewhat archly. It was meant to sound good-natured but somehow I have never managed to capture that effect.

'Well, now,' he said.

'Yes, indeed,' I replied.

He lowered his head conspiratorially and whispered, 'I didn't want to come.'

'Me neither,' I said. So at least we had one thing in common.

'How's the music coming?' he inquired gingerly.

'I don't play any more.'

'That's what Maud said, but I didn't believe her. She said you're so much like me, but I said that's not possible because I couldn't live without my cello.'

'I used to play the piano.' We both laughed.

'Don't say "used to". You'll play the piano again.'

'I really don't miss it. After all, I've had forty years of it. Remember, I was a child prodigy.'

'So was I! Didn't you know?'

I didn't. I felt like asking him if he had ever sued his parents for an accounting of his earnings.

'Of course there was that awful mess with my

parents. Much like yours, I suppose.' I wondered if he was noticing a change in my face. I could feel the blood draining from it.

I managed to stammer out, 'I didn't know about that.'

'Well, why should you?' he asked genially. 'I didn't really begin to make it on the concert stage until long after the lawsuit. I was strictly local stuff for years. I come from the Midlands, you know.' I didn't because there was no accent to betray him. 'But I did pretty damned well there for some fifteen years.' His face darkened. 'Then I met my wife. She took over from my parents. She was a concert manager.' He mentioned her name and I recognised it.

'I didn't know you were married to her.'

'Oh, yes, indeed I was. Twenty long count them years. I suppose you've heard she's left me.'

'For a flautist.'

'He's fifteen years younger than she is.'

'Then his wind's still good.' We broke up together over that one and he slapped me on the back in one of those hail-fellows-well-met gestures though my back stung for quite a while after that. We bantered back and forth amiably and jovially for at least half an hour until Maud broke it up and guided us all to the dining room. Dinner was a delicious and delightful affair and impeccably served by two white-coated young men I assumed were imported from Harrod's. Maud held court at the head of the table, and every so often I would catch her glowing with motherly pride at Tony and myself, who kept up a steady stream of chatter and jokes, batting dialogue back and forth across the table like tennis champions. I could tell that Maud considered the dinner party a huge success, the instant cameraderie between Tony and myself could only be exceeded for her by one of the Escuderos slumping over the sorbet from a heart attack which of course did not happen.

When I arrived home alone shortly after midnight, I was in amazingly good spirits. I even poured myself a brandy which is something I rarely do as brandy stimulates my adrenalin and frequently causes a sleepless night. As a matter of fact, for the first time in over a year, I played one of my own recordings and sat back in an easy chair, sipping brandy and listening to the ghost of my earlier genius. And then the phone rang.

'Good evening,' I said somewhat mockingly into the mouthpiece assuming the caller would be Maud to rehash the evening.

'Zoltan!' It was Bernice Grimshaw. 'Maud told me you were back.' Maud would. 'What the hell happened?'

I swished the brandy lazily and said, 'He was a very disappointing travelling companion.'

'Really!' You'd have thought I had slapped her in the face.

'He didn't like any of the accommodations. He complained about the food. He made snide remarks about the people we met, and he drove like a maniac.'

'Well, you're the same way, for God's sake!' Bernice should know. We once took a trip together to Majorca which was another mistake.

'I suppose so,' I said somewhat airily, 'maybe that's why I couldn't stand it. So I defected.'

'Oh, poor old Kurt,' whimpered Bernice. 'Having to drive all the way back from Scotland by his lonesome.'

'He enjoys talking to himself.'

'Oh, don't be so cruel!' she snapped. 'You're both cut from the same cloth. I should have known better than to bring you two together.'

'Don't blame yourself, dear,' I said rather wearily, 'I really didn't want to make that trip if you recall.'

'Well, I should have thought you two would have gotten along famously, whoring your way across the countryside.' Bernice was fishing for information. She was desperately in love with Kurt, who of course did not respond. He was at the mini-skirted teen-age stage, an affliction that attacks many men in their forties. I had passed through that stage myself rather swiftly.

'There wasn't very much of that, Bernice.'

'Hmmm. Well, have you any idea when he's getting back?'

'None whatsoever.'

'You men. You're absolute babies, all of you.' And Bernice wished she could diaper each and every one of us. 'Are you free for lunch tomorrow?'

'I'm sorry, but I'm not.' I wasn't lying. I was having lunch with Tony Gompers.

'I gather you and Tony Gompers got along famously tonight.' I groaned inwardly. I knew whatever she had gathered was from a crop seeded by Maud Magruder.

'I found him quite affable.' In the middle of this statement I stifled a yawn. There was no stifling Bernice.

'I'm quite friendly with his wife.' Somehow I had the feeling she was delivering a subtle warning rather than imparting an innocuous bit of information.

'Have you met her flute player?'

'I certainly have, and he's a vast improvement on Tony.'

'How can you tell? They play different instruments.'

'Don't be so snide. That's one of the reasons she finally decided to leave Tony.'

'Because I'm so snide?'

'That's almost funny. He's snide, possessive, has a

vicious temper, is given to childish tantrums, he's mean to her friends ...'

'And on the seventh day he rested.'

'Have I touched a raw nerve? It must all sound so familiar. He's so much like you.'

You're mean. You're vicious. You're vindictive. How dare you drag us through the slime like that. You're driving much too fast. Are you trying to get us killed? Are you listening? Oh, you are impossible. You're just like your father! You're so much like him!

'Bernice, it's terribly late, and I'm terribly tired.'

'What's that music I hear?'

'Liszt.'

'Seems to me I have that recording.' There was a dramatic pause followed by, 'Why it's *your* recording!'

'I only listen to the best.'

Her voice dropped an octave. 'Are you entertaining someone?'

'Myself.' I took a sip of brandy. 'We missed you at dinner tonight.'

'Oh, go to hell.'

'If you'll lead the way.' She slammed the phone down and almost gave me an earache.

As you may have gathered by now, Bernice and Maud are sisters under the skin. The catalogue of Tony's (and by inference, my) deficiencies could well apply to themselves. But I forgive them their sins as they do not forgive others. To be perfectly honest, I had planned to cancel the luncheon engagement with Tony Gompers. I know now that I don't really get along with men. I loathe sports, drinking in pubs and comparing notes on sexual victories. I suppose you're thinking that Tony and I do have music in common, but I happen to find the cello a rather unpleasant instrument. It is frequently too guttural for my taste, which is lyrical. I sometimes feel I should have studied the harp. It could have served two purposes. The second of course in my after life.

After turning off the hi-fi and swallowing my brandy, I went to bed and suffered a series of incredible nightmares. Twice I awakened in a cold sweat and briefly considered retenanting the oven right then and there. But my knees felt stiff and my nose was clogged with the symptoms of an oncoming cold, so I saw no point in wasting my time. You wonder why I don't jump off a tall building? Sadly, I have a deadly fear of heights.

In the morning over toast and coffee and *The Times* crossword puzzle (Oh not *Landseer* again!), Tony Gompers was my first phone call. I tried my cold (it really wasn't all that bad) to beg off lunch, but he's as bad as I am about rejection. He was having none of it and it finally ended up with me offering to cook lunch for the two of us. One way or another there's no avoiding that oven. Even the mean offering of eggs and sausages would not put Tony off. He insisted he wasn't much of a lunch-eater and neither am I. Oh what the hell, I decided, the hour or two will pass quickly.

Tony arrived promptly at one. To my very obvious chagrin, he was toting his cello.

'I hope you don't mind,' he said with a big smile as he followed me into the sitting room, 'there's a piece I'd like you to hear and advise me on. I composed it myself.' I could feel my spine melting. 'If you think it's any good, I'll play it at my next recital.'

'I'm not a very good judge of modern music,' I said weakly.

'You have a fine ear.' I glanced at my ear as we passed a mirror and agreed with him. 'It's a lyrical piece.' I almost stumbled en route to the kitchen. 'They don't compose enough of them for the cello, don't you think?'

'I sure do.'

The sausages were sizzling in a pan. 'Oh,' he said in an almost petulant voice, 'you fry your sausages, you don't grill them.' Little did he know how close he came to suffering a shower of sausages.

'I *always* fry sausages,' I said with a rasp as I went to the fridge for the eggs. But there was something very *deja vu* about the scene. I happen to consider myself a superior cook and have frequently been guilty of dismaying a host or hostess who hadn't prepared a dish in a manner I happen to prefer.

Tony said, through a laugh, 'I suppose you've said something similar in somebody else's kitchen at one time or another.'

Is this son of a bitch a mind reader? Can there really be such a thing as mind transference? 'Would you like a drink?'

'No, thanks, I never drink in the afternoon.'

'Neither do I.' I almost dropped an egg.

Somehow we managed to get through lunch. We had coffee in the sitting room and chatted, rather Tony chatted and I listened. He monopolised the conversation much in the way I do when I find a fresh audience. It was most discomforting. I was very much on edge and not successfully camouflaging it. I kept referring to my wristwatch and stifling yawns and picking non-existent lint from my trousers and growing bored with all the *uh-huh*'s and *I see*'s and *of course*'s I was interjecting into the conversation by way of letting him know I was still alive. There was still the cello concerto to endure. In the past, I wondered, was this the effect I had on people when I asked them to listen to a new piece I was attempting to master? Of course it was, and it frightened me. He's so much like me, and I could feel the trickle of perspiration down my side.

Just when I was about to suggest we repair to my sound-proofed studio, the phone rang. For the first time in months, I reached for it hungrily.

'Zoltan ... oh, my God, Zoltan.' It was Maud, the voice of doom.

'What's wrong, Maud. What is it?'

'Bernice just phoned. It was on the two o'clock news.'

I must have grown pale because Tony leaned forward anxiously and I averted my eyes from him. 'What was?'

'Kurt ... Kurt's been found *dead*.'

'Wha ... how ... what are you talking about?'

Maud told me Kurt's body had been found in the car in an isolated patch of woods near Aberdeen. He had apparently gone off the road during a fog and crashed into a tree. His skull had been crushed.

'How awful,' I said hoarsely.

'They say he's been dead for several days,' continued Maud at her most tragic, 'it must have happened shortly after you left him.'

'How awful,' I said again, because there was nothing else for me to say.

'But Zoltan,' Maud continued, 'the police suspect foul play.'

'How can they?' It was a stupid thing to ask, but it was the first thing that came to my mind, and I am frequently guilty of speaking the first thing that comes to my mind.

'The spanner in the trunk of the car had traces of blood on it.'

'I didn't notice when we changed the tyre. We ... we'd had a blowout going at seventy. We might have been killed. That's what brought on the argument. Oh, God. What a mess.'

'Zoltan.'

'Yes?'

'Bernice has phoned the police. She's told them you'd been travelling with Kurt.'

I fought hard to keep from exploding. Tony's curiosity was now more than piqued. His hands were making semaphores trying to get me to give him some hint of what Maud was telling me. Obviously he must have guessed Kurt was dead and under suspicious circumstances. He would have had to if he was really that much like me. 'She didn't have to do that. I would have phoned them myself.'

'Oh, darling, of all times to put you under such stress.'

'It's all right.' I was amazed at how calmly I spoke. 'It will be all right. Tony's here. We've just had lunch. Now he's going to play his new piece for me. He's brought his cello.'

Tony involuntarily was flexing his fingers.

'You're taking it beautifully,' said Maud. I might have just refused the handkerchief before the firing squad. 'Please call me later. I'm terribly concerned for you.' I promised I would and hung up. I told Tony about Kurt. All he did was shrug.

'He was a bore,' said Tony.

He shouldn't have said that. He really shouldn't have said that. I realise now Kurt was an absolute bore. And Tony Gompers is an absolute bore. So much like me, of course. I stood up abruptly and Tony followed me to the studio carrying his cello. I flung open the door and stood aside for Tony. Then I slammed the door shut and the sound it made was hollow and empty. Tony crossed to the piano and ran his fingers across the keys.

'My God this is out of tune. How could you do it to this lovely instrument?'

The veins in my temples were throbbing and I

pressed my fingers against them. Then I rubbed my sweaty palms together as Tony unpacked his cello. 'Look, Tony,' I stammered nervously, 'I don't think I could be much of a judge of anything right now. Do you mind terribly?'

He looked up at me sharply and said in a tone of voice I found offensive, 'It's a very short piece. This might be the only chance I'll get to play it for you.'

I remember wondering then why he had said something like that. It sounded in a way sadistic and I know I have sounded that way on similar occasions. I spat an epithet and moved past him to where the lithographs were stacked. I couldn't resist a deliciously nasty impulse to hang one of them while Tony tuned up the cello. I lifted the hammer, selected a nail and began pounding it into the wall.

'Well, this a fine time to do that!' Tony shouted angrily. 'Are you afraid to hear this thing because it might be too good?'

There must have been a hideous look on my face when I rounded on him, clutching the hammer. He leapt from the seat so abruptly, he stumbled over the cello and lost his balance and sprawled on to the floor.

I pounced on him like some wild animal, my left hand clutching his neck, my right arm holding the hammer poised to strike. Tony screamed and tried to scratch my face.

'Don't!' he kept shouting over again. 'Don't! Don't!'

I rained blow after blow on his skull and I could hear the bone crack as rivers of blood erupted.

'Why . . . why . . .' he gasped.

'You're so much like me!' I screamed in a voice I did not recognise. 'You're so much like me . . . *and I hate myself!*'

TIME BOMB

by Gwendoline Butler

Concerning death : it is a fact of human nature that we like deaths to be recorded. The unknown, unidentified dead disturb us. Even murderers, whether they know or not, share in this feeling, and want the names and addresses of their victims to be set down. It is often hard for them to bite back the impulse to set the record straight and they leave little messages: clues, criminologists call them. Some murderers, like Jack O'Hara, actually write their names on little cards. Even in war the anonymous dead worry people, so that afterwards they put up memorials to them.

When the bombs fell, people took refuge in caves of one sort or another. Some were man-made. One set, of natural origin, near South London, was specially favoured.

Later on, when the war was over, bodies, skeletons really, were found there. The rumour went around that they were refugees who had got trapped. This was not true, they were skeletons, but they were not products of the war, they were old, immemorially old. All the same, the stories of the skeletons were told all over the neighbourhood. Such stories cling on to life, constantly denied, never quite believed in, but never scotched either, becoming part of the folk lore of the district.

The Baker family often told it. As a girl, Mrs Margery Baker had sheltered in the caves herself and heard the story told by her dad while he was alive. She sang her children to sleep with it; surprisingly she had a sweet voice and a true ear. 'Broken bones, tick tack toe, all spread out in a row,' she sang. The children hummed with her; the sense of it did not disturb their sleep. IQs were low in the Baker family, but they were all good sleepers. However, some of the meaning must have got through, because they became a necrophilic family and even the littlest had a dry bone to rattle. Two children were exceptional, the eldest, a girl, Pauline, and a boy, Sheldon. Fancy names for fancy people.

When the third daughter and fifth child was born, Mrs Baker was put about. 'Well, I don't know,' she said to Pauline. 'You'll have to stop at home and help. You can't go to school.'

'I can't stay home, Mum,' said the practical Pauline. 'You'll have the School Attendance Officer round here, won't you? No, I'm going to school. You'll have to manage somehow during the day. I'll see to things when I get home.'

And she did. Nothing impeded her progress at school, where she was brilliant. Very soon a scholarship to a grander school came her way. 'Oh, you can't take it,' said her mother. 'We couldn't manage.'

At school Pauline said : 'I can manage about attending the school. But the uniform's the difficulty. I don't think she'd buy it.'

'We allow a grant of money.'

'Yes. I know. But *she'll* spend it and there won't be much I can do about it. I can't actually control her. No, you'll have to arrange about the uniform and I'll get myself to the school.'

So a woman from the Education Department came round and brought the uniform.

No further children born to Mrs Baker survived the first few months of life. 'A blessing really,' said the social worker who called. You weren't supposed to say this sort of thing, but she did. One or two slight bruises on the infant faces showing up after death had worried her slightly, but Mrs Baker seemed genuinely distressed, the deaths were otherwise natural and, as she thought, were a blessing really.

The second child, Sheldon, grew up. Science was his special bent; he was even more brilliant than his sister and soon won an even grander scholarship to a great school. The same problem came.

'You'll have to work it the way I did,' Pauline advised him. 'I'll send for the Education Officer.'

The woman from the city's Education Office and the social worker met on the stairs.

'These children's maternal grandfather was Jack O'Hara.' It was something she had long wanted to get out. 'He did away with twenty-three people before they caught up with him. All from the best of motives, of course. Or so he said.'

Jack O'Hara, the most celebrated mass murderer of all time. Other men, in Dusseldorf and Hamburg and Chicago, had put away more, but none had his style. He always laid his victims out neatly and put their name, if he knew it and he nearly always did, on a card on their breast, with his signature appended.

'The rest of the family are dregs, but these two children are worth saving.'

'I knew about Jack O'Hara,' admitted the woman from the Education Office. 'I think about it every time I meet them. I'm glad you spoke.'

'It makes you think,' said the social worker. 'They're a very cohesive family, though. Hang together.' She gave an uneasy laugh. The image of *all* the Baker family hanging together, like dead dolls, disturbed her. 'Take Dad now. I don't know what function Dad's got in the family, but I swear they're fond of him.'

'What sort's Dad?'

'He eats and drinks. Drinks quite a lot, takes what jobs he can get, loses them mostly.'

Mrs Baker had one treasure which was a heavy brass ornament which had belonged to her mother and grandmother and which she kept well polished. Pauline told her no, it was not a vase, it was a First World War shell case and would once have been full of high explosive.

When Pauline was seventeen she won a scholarship to Oxford; her brother, unusually talented as a mathematician, won one to an equally famous university. Pauline saw to the arrangements.

'The Education Office say they will pay the money grants direct into our own bank accounts,' she announced briskly.

'So we're independent?'

Pauline nodded.

'What about *them*?' He meant the others, the rest of the family.

'Ah, that's it, isn't it?' They looked at each other. 'They're getting worse, aren't they?' Sheldon nodded. 'Mum always polishing her brass. And Dad – have you noticed they've started drinking now? That's new. I used to think as the kids grew up and things got easier they'd learn how to manage. But it's not so. It must be something deeper in them than I'd thought. And the kids! The little one really *can't* walk and she's never going to.'

Sheldon cleared his throat. 'We can't leave them.'

'No.' She was decisive. Their eyes met.

They took vacation jobs. They didn't need to consult each other about the jobs they took, she in a chemist's shop, he driving a van.

In early October, two weeks before their University

term started, Pauline said: 'We're going to move you, Mother. To a much better home. Tell Mrs Welsh next door. Let her have the furniture. I'm getting you all new.'

Mrs Baker was excited, she liked the idea of a move. Mrs Welsh agreed with her. 'They're good kids, your two eldest,' said Mrs Welsh. 'You got good kids, Mrs Baker.'

They moved late one evening. Pauline made them a last hot drink in the old house, the three other children, her mother and dad. 'Hot cocoa,' she said. 'Make you sleep.'

It should; some hundreds of tablets of pheno-barbitone were crushed in it.

'I like thick cocoa,' said Dad. 'Reminds me of my days in the Navy. The King's Navy it was then.'

'You were only in the Navy two days, Dad,' said Pauline tolerantly. 'Then they discovered you had fits.' She poured him an extra large mug of cocoa; it was all calculated scientifically according to body weight, and he was a large man.

'I'll have a little more if I may, Pauly.'

She shook her head. 'Enough is enough. I've got it all worked out.'

Pauline arranged Mother, Father, brothers and sisters in the van. Sheldon drove. She sat by him. Everyone in the back of the van was quiet.

'They've found the rum,' said Pauline.

'Mum didn't take much of the cocoa.'

'Enough I think. She's got good resistance, has Mum, but she's taking plenty of the rum. That'll do the job.'

'What was she fiddling round in the back of the van for?'

'Was she? I didn't see.'

They travelled in silence. Sheldon knew where he was going.

'Here we are, Mum,' said Pauline eventually, helping her mother out of the back of the van. 'Mind the path.'

'Oh, are we going to the caves, Pauly?' said her mother, dreamily. 'Where's Dad? I'm afraid the little ones have dropped off.'

'He's coming. Sheldon's helping him.'

'I've always liked the caves. Remember how I used to tell you stories about sheltering there? Are we going to live here?'

'Yes. Right at the back. You're going to be a troglodyte.'

'I believe I shall like that.'

'I think you will, Mum.'

'But won't people come looking? I like to be private.'

'You'll be private. No one's going to come here.'

Dad didn't speak. He'd had more of the rum. Pauline and Sheldon conducted their parents to a little cul de sac on one side of the caves, and made them comfortable on rugs. They tucked the family in, put out all but one candle and got into the van.

'It was the only way,' said Pauline. 'They'll be quite safe there. For always.'

'Yes. We had to do what was best for them,' agreed Sheldon. He started the van. 'And after all, we have our own lives to live. I left an envelope with their names and addresses in Dad's pocket. But, of course, they'll never be found.'

In the cave Mrs Baker shifted herself on her blankets. 'I suppose I'm in bed. Dad, you've gone very quiet. Isn't it funny, Dad, I've never felt happier or freer. Wonderful kids,' she said sleepily.

In the dim dark distance there was a faint bang, almost like a bomb. The cave reverberated softly.

'Remember how we used to come here during the war, Dad, because of the bombs? You know *my* bomb, Dad? A shell case from the first World War, Pauline said it was. Blood, sweat and tears, that's what Churchill said, wasn't it? That was another war, you used to say. I fairly loved that brass. But think of it quietly living there, all alone, all through Granny's day, through my mother's, through my life, two wars. Stop polishing that useless brass, you used to say. You can never tell when things are going to be useful.'

She went on in a whisper.

'I knew my brass wasn't dead. There was a bit of powder still in it at the bottom. TNT, I said to myself, that's a name I know. I never told you. Not Pauline. Nor Sheldon. And today I saw that look in their eyes. The look like my Dad's ... I put a piece of petrol soaked rag inside the brass and set light to it so it would smoulder and I hid the brass inside the van. The heat will grow and grow and the powder will feel it ...'

Perhaps Dad was not so far gone as might have been supposed. At any rate, there was a faint mutter. 'Wouldn't work, love. Like all your ideas. Know you do your best, but not a chance. Wouldn't do. Silly old girl.' It was her epitaph. His too.

Outside in the night air the van was hurrying away. The two in front smelt burning and Pauly turned round and swore. 'Bit of an old rag burning,' she said.

'Doing any harm?'

'It's catching light to some paper. Nothing else.' She leaned over to beat the fire out. She could have put it out easily, it was nothing of a fire, but in her haste she pushed against the driver. The car swerved, driving like a bomb straight at a lorry loaded with cement.

'Did you hear that bang, Dad? I think that bang was it. That was Pauly and Sheldon going up.'

But there was no bang except in her mind, their death was swift and accompanied only by the sound of tearing metal. They predeceased their mother by some minutes. As she knew.

'After all,' she said, as she turned easily into her eternal sleep. 'I couldn't let them grow up like Dad, could I?'

TURN AND TURN ABOUT

by Francis Clifford

When he first set eyes on her she was billed as *L'Oiseau D'Or* and she was seventy feet above his head at a tented circus near Madrid. Now he called her Tony, short for Antonia, and she knew him simply as Clay – that, and no more. They never went far with names. She was as small-boned and beautiful and daring as a bird, and within seconds of seeing her he had felt for sure that she was the one for him.

'What are you doing with the rest of your life?' – old movies have such lines. Yet these were the words he'd used, and only five weeks ago. Since when the two of them had discovered the seclusion of this rented salt-white villa perched amid the spectacular coastal scenery of Sardinia. 'Love me, bird girl?' he would ask and, as often as not, she would wrinkle her nose and frown a bit and pretend to give it serious consideration.

She was, he guessed, in her very early twenties. Her hands were enormously expressive, compensating for occasional lapses in her slightly accented English. Her mother, he learned, was Spanish and her father came from Poland; both were circus people, still active with a juggling routine somewhere in the States. She had Modigliani eyes, brown, wonderfully alert, and her straight raven-dark hair was shoulder length. What her surname was she had never told him, and it didn't matter; Tony was label enough.

'Tony,' Clay said now, watching her, 'you're gorgeous.'

'Thank you.'

'More so every day.'

'You are a great flatter.'

'Flatter*er*,' he corrected.

'You're so clever, and I'm a dense.'

'Dunce.'

'All right, but a dunce in four languages.' The line of her lips was tighter than she realised. 'At least I am not a prisoner of my tongue, like you and all the other English.'

He grimaced amiably. '*Touché.*' Then he kissed her.

'Give me a cigarette, will you?'

Clay lit one and transferred it direct to her mouth. They were by the pool, stretched out on loungers. Olive skin and pink bikini – every time he ran his eyes over her he marvelled. He was thirty years old, stocky and muscular. His hair was short and crinkled, his eyes blue. Only an enemy could have suggested he was anything but handsome. He had told her he was a Londoner, which made straightforward sense, and explained that he was in the metal business – 'exclusively non-ferrous' – which didn't interest her enough to question whether it made sense or not.

'How about a drink?'

'Please,' she said. 'A Cloudy Sky.'

'Does that mean gin and ginger beer?'

He got up and began to pad around the pool's edge. 'Know something?' he said, turning his head. 'You're a gift, bird girl. A pure gift.'

He slipped as the last word left his mouth. For a few seconds he was all arms and legs, wildly trying to retain his balance. Finally, like a drunken dancer, he pirouetted on the wet tiles and crashed down.

'Clay! . . . Are you all right?'

For a moment he didn't move. Then he pushed himselm into a sitting position.

'All right?'

He nodded. She began to laugh, head back. But when she looked at him again his face was contorted and he was gripping both ankles.

'Clay —'

'Wow.' His eyes widened with pain. '*Wow* . . .'

'What is it?' She squatted anxiously beside him. 'Broken?'

'Shouldn't think so.'

'I'll call a doctor.'

'Let's get up first.'

He struggled on to the nearest lounger and gingerly explored the damage.

'Well?'

'Really turned them over, didn't I?' He sucked in air between clenched teeth. 'Left one's not so bad. But the right – ayeeeee . . .'

Her hands fluttered. 'Is it bones?'

'Bones, no. Muscles, ligaments.'

'Muscles – ah.'

She rose at once and went into the house. When she came back she carried an ice bucket and a wad of table napkins. She wrapped crushed ice in a napkin and draped the compress gently round Clay's right ankle.

He said : 'You've done this before.'

'In a circus these things happen.'

'Hardly with my flair and style.'

'We are not all with your talent.'

'Bitch,' he said.

'Now you have to take it easy and look at the view.'

'I know all about the view. I've seen it before.'

'Only robbers and gipsies say you must never return. Which one of those are you?'

'Of all the bloody things to have happened ... Tony, girl, you're looking at a prize idiot.'

'I know it.'

'All done by – ouch! – mirrors. Incredible, isn't it? Nothing up my sleeves.'

She slid away from him, pushing a cushion under the extended leg. 'You need to keep it high.'

'Is that so?'

'And tonight, if it isn't any better —'

'Tonight, if it isn't any better, the nurse will be in trouble.'

'Tonight,' she smiled, 'if it isn't any better, your problems will be to catch the nurse.'

'I'll manage,' Clay said.

'It would not surprise me.'

He winced slightly. 'You, bird girl, are a great flatter.'

Later in the afternoon she drove the Fiat to the village. It was a corkscrew stretch of road, narrow and unpredictable, offering head-on glimpses of the sea one moment and mountain views the next. Figs and olives grew on the bordering slopes and goats scattered as the car passed, tyres sobbing through the turns.

'Take it easy,' Clay had muttered, half asleep as she left him. 'There's no safety-net out there.'

The village was piled around a small fishing harbour. A week ago, when Tony first appeared with her raffia basket and walked barefooted in trousers and bikini-top, the locals had no idea that anyone so desirably symmetrical could bring such drama and passion to the purchase of a few daily commodities. But word had since spread, and now she was greeted with respect as well as wonder.

Once or twice a week a coachload of crab-red tourists

arrived and sampled the sucking pig at the restaurant on the quayside and ate the unleavened bread and went away; but today the village was spared. Tony finished her shopping and turned along the waterfront. Strangers nodded as she passed and she acknowledged each in turn. When she reached the restaurant she unslung the basket from her shoulder and seated herself at one of the tables on the paved area outside.

'*Un cappuccino.*'

She lit a cigarette and glanced at *La Stampa*. Only a handful of people were there – a blue-chinned priest intent on his office, a couple of middle-aged women, heads close together, a powerful-looking man with the *Herald-Tribune* and a lip-line moustache who couldn't keep his eyes away from her. The coffee came and she added sugar. The world's news was as depressing as ever and she didn't dwell on it. She smoked the cigarette through, crumbled a biscuit for the pigeons, smiled to herself at the memory of Clay's involuntary fandango, paid the bill and left, retracing her steps to where she had parked the car.

Less than an hour after setting out she swung into the villa's short steep driveway. It had just gone five o'clock and the brassy glare had left the sky. She hauled her basket off the seat and made for the front door.

'Hold it!'

Startled, she turned. It was the man from the restaurant. As fast as light she wondered how on earth he could have got there so soon. And in the self-same instant she saw he had a pistol.

He was wearing a crumpled light-weight suit and carried an airline travel bag. With heightened awareness she noted his coarse brown thinning hair and the blue and white sweatshirt under his jacket.

He jerked the gun. 'Take me through.'

She wheeled around and did exactly as he said, opening the iron-studded door and leading him into the apparent darkness of the house. There was a yawning sensation in the pit of her stomach and, as they emerged on to the terrace beside the pool, the villa had never seemed so isolated. Clay was dozing, shaded by an umbrella, oblivious of his vulnerability.

'Who else is here?' the man said, right on her heels.

'Nobody.'

'No maid?'

'No.'

'Gardener? ... Dog?'

'No.'

The questions were over-loud, and Clay stirred. He opened his eyes and gazed at them both with bleary affability.

'Hallo,' he said. 'You caught me napping.' Then he saw the gun and his expression changed. He sat up as if he'd been stung. 'What the hell —?'

'Stay where you are.'

'Who are you?' Clay squeezed his eyes against the light, bewildered now. Things like this happened to other people. 'What's going on, for Christ's sake?'

'He was outside,' Tony faltered. 'He was waited for me.'

'Go and join him,' the man said. He used his head like a boxer. 'Get yourself over there and speak when you're spoken to.'

He was on the tall side, broad with it, all muscle. His accent was hard yet back in the throat. Whatever he was it probably wasn't American and certainly wasn't English.

To Tony he said : 'Why's flatfoot got the bandage?'

'He twist his ankle.'

'Oh yes?' The gun gave him complete authority. He came round the end of the pool. 'Fine time for it to happen.'

'Listen —' Clay began.

'You've got it inside out. My listening days are dead and gone.'

'What the bloody hell d'you want?'

'We're coming to that,' the man said. He sat on the edge of the second lounger, very sure of himself, looking them over. He put the travel bag down between his feet and took off his jacket, transferring the gun from hand to hand. His sinewy forearms were mahogany-brown; on one was tattooed MORGEN and on the other GESTERN. 'We're going to do each other a good turn, you and the girl and me.'

'We don't need any good turns.'

'The fact remains that when I say jump you're going to jump. When I say move you're going to move ... Like now, for instance. By way of example.' He stood up and nodded at Tony. 'It's time you showed me around.'

She frowned.

'I want to see the house. And while we're inside,' he warned Clay, 'don't try anything foolish. Otherwise it'll be the worse for her, and I've no wish for that. My part of this deal's to cause you no harm.'

Tony led him into the villa. He was as quiet as a cat behind her. In the living room she checked between strides for her vision to adjust and felt the gun touch her spine.

'Where's the telephone?'

She took him to the main bedroom. She pushed the door open and stood aside, but he signalled her to go on through. 'What is the idea?' she began, white showing in her eyes, but the moment passed. He rounded the bed and ripped the telephone from the wall, a kind of savagery in the way it was done, as if to frighten from her mind any lingering suspicion that none of this was really happening.

He made a swift tour of the other rooms, not a word spoken, never more than a yard or two between them. In the kitchen he took a beer from the ice-box and drank it from the can; in the garage he showed passing interest in the rubber suits and aqualungs. Otherwise he didn't pause. Within minutes he was prodding her out on to the terrace again and Clay was staring at them both with sullen impotence.

'There's a sensible guy,' the man said. 'Congratulations.' The sun jazzed on the surface of the pool. 'Ever seen a marionette show?' He produced what amounted to a grin. 'The crudest pressures are the best – wouldn't you say that?'

'You're a bastard.'

There was no reaction. He went where he had left the travel bag and tore the zip across. He reached inside and took out a walkie-talkie radio; it was black with white metal trim and had a shoulder strap fitment.

He said to Tony: 'What d'you make of it?'

'I don't make.'

'Specially designed for those who are out of sight but not out of mind.'

'I don't understand.'

'You will.' He took a second handset from the bag and pressed a red button; three feet of telescopic aerial extended with a series of soft clicks. 'Know how these things function?'

Tony shook her head.

'Come and learn.'

She met his gaze. 'And if I say no?'

'You don't look that stupid.'

'I am not stupid enough to have printings on my arms, either.' Her anger flared, out of control. 'Morgen and gestern – tomorrow and yesterday ... What is it supposed to mean? Only peoples who have never grown up have words and pictures on their skin.'

The man let fly, the point of his shoe making contact with Clay's injured ankle. Clay yelped and twisted away, his mouth an O.

'See what trouble you can cause?' the man said reprovingly. 'Your friend could have done without that.' His tone changed. 'Get hold of that second handset and listen to me.'

Reluctantly she picked it up. He began to explain how to operate it: nothing could have been more simple and she had no questions. The gun was always in evidence, utterly persuasive. Once or twice she glanced at Clay, conveying alarm as well as defeat. The man told her to go to the far end of the terrace and make contact, *sotto voce*, from there. After several false starts and shouted instructions to push the SPEAK or LISTEN switch their exchanges became reasonably proficient. Tony finally came through with: 'Whatever you want we are not your kind of peoples. You made a mistake picking this house ... Over.'

'I never said to push your luck ... Over.'

'You are a bad dream.' She was as petulant as a child. 'Over.'

'I'm flesh-and-blood real, and you know it ... Over and out.'

'For Christ's sake,' Clay tried again. 'Who the hell are you? Half an hour ago —'

'Half an hour ago, flatfoot, you were a non-contributing member of society. Once upon a girl's a good time, and so say all of us, but there's more to life than lotus-eating. Very soon now you're going to make your-self useful.'

Tony walked towards them. 'You are all hot air.' She was never able to hold her tongue. 'All talk, all the time talk.'

'Is that how it seems?'

'I think you are one big bluff.'

The man fired into the space between Clay and her-self. The gun spat and jumped in his hand and a beach-ball exploded behind them – all in an echo-less split second, so fast they hardly flinched. A fraction after-wards they blinked, caught their breath, stiffened; and a moment later the shrivelled casing of the ball slapped into the pool.

'God almighty,' Clay whispered. In terms of the bullet's path about two feet separated him from Tony; no more. The back of his neck prickled, ice and fire.

'Don't put faith in the bluff idea,' the man said. 'You'll only regret it ... Let's have that understood once and for all. There's just the three of us and we might as well be together in a locked room.'

A bougainvillaea-covered balustrade enclosed the near end of the pool. He crossed over to it, cryptic and shatteringly offhand, and looked out at the savage beauty of the scene beyond. Once upon a time the face of an entire mountainside had crumbled into the sea. Fantastic heaps of weathered rock now shaped the coast-line, and the sea itself lay green and azure and gentian in a score of bays. The village was fudge-coloured in the near distance, and here and there were scattered a few medium-size villas, perched dramatically between sea and mountain, their stark newness redeemed by tamarisks and myrtle and splashes of flowers.

'Come and join me,' the man said. 'You, too, flat-foot. And bring the bag.'

With difficulty Clay hopped across, unable to equate the man's conversational style with his reckless use of the gun, imprisoned momentarily in disbelief about himself and Tony and their situation.

'You'll find binoculars in the bag,' he was told. 'And a tripod. Let's have them out.'

He had no choice. Despite their size the binoculars were surprisingly light.

'Try them.'

He sighted on the villa known as Castello di Roccia. In all respects it was a place apart, incomparable in size and setting, rising sheer from the very tip of a narrow finger of land which separated one bay from another. Its stucco was the palest of blues, its huge area of ribbed roof a reddish brown. Terraced gardens faced inland and a raised driveway led to wrought-iron gates set in high colour-washed walls. Clay fiddled the soft blur into focus and the detail leapt at him across a quarter of a mile, fantastically sharp and clear.

'Good, eh?'

Against his will Clay nodded.

'Steady it on the tripod and you'll find it's almost too good to be true.'

Sunlight lay across the sea like a bar of molten metal and the sea itself was a travel-brochure blue. The boat Clay used for water-skiing was moored in the horseshoe bay below.

'Listen,' the man said as lightly as if they were playing a game. 'Who's heard of the Rivers diamond?'

Clay and Tony exchanged glances, but neither answered.

'Don't you read the magazines?' He was close, standing back a little, but the gun made him safe. 'No? ... You're education's incomplete. For your information the Rivers diamond is one of the big ones.'

'So what?' Clay frowned.

'The Rivers diamond,' the man said evenly, 'belongs to a certain Barbara Ashley. And the Barbara Ashley in question —'

'God,' Clay exclaimed, anticipating.

'– lives in the Castello di Roccia. And the Castello di Roccia, as you very well know, is straight in front of you.'

Something seemed to heave in Tony's brain. She looked first at the man, then at Clay, then back to the man, transferring the same startled glance.

'Why are you tell us this?'

'Because,' the man said, 'I want the Rivers diamond for myself ... And you're the one who's going to get it for me.'

Time seemed to miss a beat.

'*Me?*'

'Correct.'

'You're crazy.' Tony tossed her head, incredulity in her voice. 'I never hear such nonsense talk.'

'You're getting it, beautiful, and that's that.'

'How?' She fluttered her hands. 'How? ... It isn't possible. Besides —'

'It's possible, all right.'

'Not by me.'

'You better than anyone.'

Clay said: 'You must be out of your mind. She isn't a thief.'

'There's always a first time. ... Give her the glasses,' the man said curtly, 'and let her see where she's going.'

'You can't make her.'

'You know damn well I can, so shut up ... Now,' he said with a nod at Tony, 'take a long look – and listen like you've never listened before.'

She lifted the binoculars to her eyes. He gave her almost half a minute to herself before speaking again.

'There's only one normal way in – along the driveway and through the gates. But that's hardly for you; Barbara Ashley doesn't exactly keep open house. And if you go over the wall you'll find the garden's alive with guards. What's more you'll still be outside the house. So you won't do anything like that.'

She glanced sideways at Clay, appalled, tongue-tied.

'Keep looking,' the man went on. 'Look left, all the way left as far as the cliff edge. See the wall there? – like an extension of the cliff itself?' He waited, restless as a guide. 'Right across from that cliff-edge part of the wall are two balconied windows on the second floor of the house . . . Got them? – between the casuarinas.'

He took her silence for assent.

'The windows are the Ashley woman's dressing room and bathroom – from left to right respectively. Nothing else need interest you.'

To Tony it seemed they were almost close enough to reach out and touch. Yet in reality they were an almost impossible goal. In a voice that didn't sound much like her own she heard herself say: 'This must be all a joke . . . Some kind of a joke.'

'Ten seconds inside that dressing room – that's all you'll need.'

'I could never get there.'

'A little help from me and flatfoot, and you'll surprise yourself.'

'Never,' she said. 'Never.'

'Tonight,' the man continued relentlessly, 'it's party time somewhere over Calagonone way – and the invitations include you-know-who. No ordinary party, believe me. The strongroom at the bank's already been visited with the occasion in mind. Which means that

until the gates open and the white Mercedes drives her
away the stuff I've set my sights on is in the villa for the
taking.'

'Tonight?' – this was Clay.

'Tonight, yes.'

'Where did you hear all this?' Disbelief still
sharpened his tone. 'How in the hell —?'

'I've got friends.'

'Not here you haven't.'

'Here,' the man said, 'I've got accomplices.'

Tony wheeled on him. 'Why me?' She gestured
almost pleadingly. 'Why us?'

'Listen,' he said. 'When it's time we'll take the boat
across to the base of the cliff. The two of us, yes ...
We climb the cliff together, descend together, return
together. The only time you'll travel alone is from the
top of the wall to the dressing room and back again –
and even then you'll have flatfoot whispering in your
ear.'

Clay scowled. 'I don't get you.'

'You'll guide her in by walkie-talkie. And the instructions you give will depend on what you see
through the Zeiss. The requirement is an empty
dressing room and with lighted windows and those
binoculars you'll as good as have your own key-hole.'

'Suppose the curtains are drawn?'

'They never are. She leaves the windows open, too.'

'How d'you know?'

Again the man said: 'Friends.' He lifted his
shoulders. 'Observation ... What are friends for?' He
seemed grimly amused. 'Barbara Ashley moves from
dressing room to bathroom, then back to the dressing
room again. Habit points to the dressing room being
unoccupied for fifteen to twenty minutes. That's when
you two come into your own. The rest will be roses.'

Tony had lowered the binoculars. She was pale and strained. 'Those guards you talk about ...'

'We've cheated them already.'

'There is garden between the wall and that part of the house, the same as other places.'

'Take another look,' the man ordered. Then: 'What else d'you see?'

'Where?'

'From high wall to window.'

'Telephone wires?'

'Right first time ... Just waiting for you to give a command performance.'

Her eyes as she turned were wide with amazement, but for seconds on end it was as if she had lost her voice. 'Do you mean ...?' she faltered, got no further and tried again. 'Do you seriously mean ...?'

The man filled the hanging silence. 'Why else d'you think I'm here, beautiful? They may not know it down in the village, but you're a very clever girl.'

'Those wires would never hold me.'

'Want to bet on it?'

'You bastard,' Clay said with useless venom.

The gun made it all inevitable. The man's changes of mood were unpredictable, but there were going to be no deviations from his plan; that was a certainty.

'I singled you out,' he told them, 'and I've chosen my time. Don't kid yourselves along with fancy ideas that I might decide to cut and run. This operation's going ahead just the way you've been told.'

Tony had no illusions left: the incredible was happening and she was a part of it. They watched the day die behind the purple mountainside. Bats began to flit and darkness spread like a stain across the water. The lamps of the distant village trembled brightly under the early stars. The Castello di Roccia seemed suspended between sea and sky, its shadowy bulk pierced by a dozen lighted windows. Clay had the binoculars trained on the only two that mattered; lit up and enlarged they offered astonishing detail. 'Like I told you,' the man said. 'You'll be a regular Peeping Tom, so take care your attention doesn't wander.' He made them practise with the walkie-talkie, sending Tony out into the night, extending the range. 'Stay out of touch for more than thirty seconds and flatfoot's going to wish he never set eyes on you.'

She kept slavishly in touch, and she came back. 'Like a lamb,' the man said, arrogantly confident. He showed no sign of nerves, but Tony suffered – chain-smoking, unable to remain still. At eight fifteen he got her to rope Clay to a chair set behind the tripod-mounted binoculars, and at half past he followed Tony down the rocky slope to where the boat was. They were wearing the rubber suits from the garage and were soon invisible. His parting words to Clay were: 'Don't go silent on us, flatfoot. Don't ever let me get the idea you're trying to be smart.'

He had no trouble with the outboard; one swing and it fired. He nosed out into the bay, throttled back and running quiet, handling the boat with a sure touch. Once they reached the open water he cut the engine and fitted the oars and made Tony row.

Quite soon he said to Tony: 'Ask flatfoot if he can see us.'

She called Clay, her voice low and surly. She had the walkie-talkie slung like a bandolier.

'Yes and no,' Clay reported. 'Only because there's a reason to look.'

'Can you hear us?'

'No.'

The sea was dead calm. Tony rowed them steadily past their own blunt headland and started in a wide arc across the next bay, traces of phosphorescence in the water, the cliff they would scale already looming, the villa on its summit already blocking out the lowermost stars. At most it took about fifteen minutes to reach the base of the cliff, during which Clay must have reported all of a dozen times. 'Dressing room and bathroom empty ... No one there yet ... Still empty, still no one there ...' Only once was his whisper distorted, sucked away; otherwise he might have been with them.

The man steered the boat with uncanny precision, never hesitating, reading the darkness with impressive assurance. How he did it Tony neither knew nor cared; to the exclusion of everything else her thoughts were congealed around what awaited her at the top of the cliff.

'Both rooms still empty ...'

Presently there was a soft grating sound. All at once the darkness was solid to the touch and they could smell the weed growths. The man grunted and ordered Tony to ship the oars. He worked the boat along with his hands. After about twenty yards they slid into a resonant gap beneath a flying buttress of rock where the water was as still as a pool. He made fast there, fore and aft, then clambered on to a ledge, hauling Tony after him. She could hardly see an inch and accepted his help, unconscious of the irony. Together they moved crabwise along the shelf until they were out from under the buttress and on the cliff face itself.

'Straight up.'

She hesitated.

'You first.' Even now he couldn't resist a jibe. 'What kind of fool d'you take me for?'

She began to climb. To her relief it was easier, less

sheer, than she'd imagined. She had no fear of heights and there were holds everywhere, hand and foot. Almost the worst thing on the way were the reports from Clay which prodded her mind where it least wanted to go.

'No one in either room ...'

She lost track of time. Once or twice something broke off and rattled down. She was breathing hard and so was the man. When she looked up the stars thudded in and out of focus with every beat of her heart. Eventually she reached the top and lay there panting. The villa's wall stood several yards from the edge like a massive cake decoration. She stared at it, thinking back, thinking forward, no prospect of refusal or defiance remaining in her. Somehow it had come to this.

'The crudest pressures are the best ...' *Madre de Dios*. 'Do what he wants,' Clay had urged anxiously. 'He's trigger-happy. Try it, for Pete's sake ...' All right. *All right*.

Presently she climbed on to the man's shoulders and hauled herself up on to the wall. It was incredibly quiet and she moved with immense caution. A narrow width of the shrub-filled garden lay between her and the house. The balconied windows she had last seen through the Zeiss were off to her right, ablaze with light and partly hidden by trees, and she edged along to bring herself nearer, on the look-out for the telephone wires.

Without warning someone cleared his throat and spat. She froze, scared out of her mind, the pulsing seconds stretched into great distortions of time. At last she spotted movement – a dark figure passing away from her, patrolling a path under the lee of the house. She waited, flattened on top of the wall, until the figure had gone from view, and an enormous effort was required to force herself on again.

It was only a short while before she saw the twin wires. They stretched from above the dressing-room balcony to a gibbet-type post planted just inside the wall; the gleam of glass insulators located them for her. She began to work her way closer, dry in the mouth, still unable to see into the windows because of the trees.

But suddenly a shadow blinked the light from inside. And, almost simultaneously, Clay was through on the walkie-talkie.

'She's in the room now.'

Clay watched Barbara Ashley enter the dressing room and start to disrobe. She was a well-built blonde in her late thirties with three husbands already dead and a millionaire fourth just divorced. In other circumstances it might have given him pleasure. Twice she flitted in and out of the bathroom. Once, half naked, she stood before an ornate mirror and held a heavy pendant to her neck.

'Still there.'

He was terse and to the point. He had had no glimpse of Tony and, since she called him from the boat, there had been no word from her either. It was beginning to seem as if he was talking to himself. Fretting, he pressed the SPEAK switch yet again.

'Still there.'

Barbara Ashley chose that precise moment to step out of her pants and saunter more positively into the adjoining bathroom. Clay waited, allowing her a chance to change her mind. If Tony made a false start across the wires it could be disastrous. He delayed for at least a couple of minutes before coming to a decision.

'All clear ... You can go now.'

Once more he had this feeling that nobody listened. He screwed his eyes to the binoculars. A long time seemed to pass without anything happening and the beginnings of alarm stirred in his guts. Then, dramatically, he saw Tony silhouetted in space as she approached the window on the wires, small and compact, arms outstretched like a Balinese dancer. An exclamation escaped him. He watched as if mesmerised. She progressed with unnerving slow-motion and he sweated for her, the tension agonising. In a circus they would have been straining to applaud.

Eventually she came close enough to the balcony to be able to lower herself on to it. For a short while before she reappeared in front of the window she was lost to him against the dark of the house. The urge was to contact her, encourage her, but he fought it down. She darted like a shadow along the balcony, stopped, hesitated, then opened the window. A moment later she was inside and he held his breath as she hurried across the room, sharing the knife-edge seconds with her.

'Not only the Rivers,' the man had said. 'The rest as well.'

It astonished Clay how quickly she emerged. He supposed the jewellery was on the table from which Barbara Ashley had picked up the pendant; at any rate Tony didn't have to look far. She came out, busily stuffing something inside her rubber suit. It was child's play – except for the wires. Her return crossing started him sweating again. Half way over she suddenly stopped in her tracks, her silhouette absolutely motionless, and he guessed a guard was near. He pressed against the ropes, imagination on the rampage. When she finally moved again he began to tremble with relief, and by the time he reckoned she was off the wires and over the wall and on the way down the cliff relief had changed to exultation.

He continued his watch on the window. Barbara Ashley took her time in the bathroom and the boat was almost back at its mooring before she came out and theatrically discovered her loss. In fact Clay heard the boat throbbing softly into the small bay below at the self-same moment as the distant dumb-show panic in the Castello di Roccia got under way.

He waited impatiently for Tony and the man to arrive from the horseshoe beach. It was almost over; the future was about to begin again. After a while an area of darkness seemed to shift and he made out Tony on the path. But nobody else. Only Tony, walking up the path alone.

'Where is he?'

Even then he expected the man to answer. He peered past her, braced for the bullying voice.

'Where is he?'

'He won't be coming.'

She was though the gate on to the terrace. 'Not coming? How d'you mean?' There and then it seemed about the most unbelievable thing he'd ever heard. '*Why* isn't he coming?'

'Because I left him there,' she said.

His mouth was hanging open as she flopped into the chair beside him.

'What d'you mean – "left him there"?'

'He is at the bottom of the cliff.'

An awful thought struck him. 'Alive?'

'Of course alive.'

'God,' he said.

His brain seemed to have gone numb. He shot a glance across the water. Someone at the Castello di

Roccia had switched on the floodlighting.

'He has what he deserve,' Tony was saying. 'Give me some cognac, please.'

'How can I?' She seemed to have forgotten that he was bound to the chair. 'Tony – what happened? For Pete's sake what happened?'

'I stole a lot of things, that's what happen.'

He shook his head frantically. 'To him.' He was repeating himself. 'What happened to him?'

'I gave him a push ... Right at the finish, when we are both in the boat and the boat is not tied up, I gave him a push and drove off.'

'Oh my God,' Clay said.

'He was swearing something awful.'

Clay swallowed. 'Get me out of all this.' She started to loosen the ropes. 'What about the stuff you took?'

'He's got it.'

'Oh my God.'

'Not again.'

'Huh?'

'That's all you say – oh my God this, oh my God that.' She freed the last knot and flipped the rope aside. 'Get me the cognac, Clay.'

'But that man —'

'Excuse me, but I have been up a cliff and over some bad wires and into someone else's room and down a cliff —'

'And incriminated yourself ... Me as well.' He was on his feet. 'Of all the damn stupid things to have done. Don't you see? We're in trouble unless he gets away – both of us.'

'I was made to steal. He force me. And you were tied up.'

'Try telling the police that.'

'It's the truth.'

'Not the kind of truth they'll believe.'

Clay went quickly to the binoculars and trained them on the base of the cliff, but he might as well have been staring into a dark tunnel. He straightened, agitated, urgency in every move he made.

'I'll have to go get him.'

'You'll *what*?'

'We're sunk if he's found.'

'Sunk . . . What is sunk?'

'To hell with that now,' he snapped. 'I'm going. Keep a look-out for me.'

He picked up the walkie-talkie he'd been using and started towards the gate. Tony made a final show of bewildered protest.

'You're crazy. The way he treated you and me.'

'That's not the point.'

'It is ridiculous to have all that again.'

'He won't come back here.'

'If he still has the gun you will have to take him where he wants.'

'All he'll want will be to get away. I'll dump him somewhere along the coast.'

'Why not let him swim?'

He wasn't listening any more. She got up and went to the balustrade and looked over, watching the night swallow him up as he hurried away. Her eyes narrowed in the star-green darkness.

'What happen to your ankle?' She'd intended waiting until later, but she couldn't resist it. 'All of a sudden you lost your limp.'

She went into the house and poured herself a cognac and got out of the rubber suit. She hadn't the slightest doubt about what she was going to do. Less than five minutes later she was in the Fiat and on the road. Half way to the village a couple of cars crammed with *cara-binieri* screamed by in the other direction. Around the next bend she pulled on to the verge and switched the engine off.

'Clay?' she said softly into the walkie-talkie. 'Clay?'
He was soon there. 'Yes?'
'The police are on their way ... Over.'
'Right.'
'... You found your friend yet?'
He parried it well. 'Friend?' She could hear the muffled engine beat.
'Partner, then.'
'What are you driving at?'
'You know ...'
'... Sounds to me you're off your head.'
'Not any longer ... flatfoot.' Her lips curled. 'Are you still listen?' She kept the thing on SPEAK. 'Tell your friend he made one big mistake. Those printings on his skin – morgen and gestern. I saw those once before. The face I'd forgot, but not the printings – or where I saw them ... It was in Madrid. He was reading a poster of *L'Oiseau D'Or* and it was the same day you later came and said to me "Hallo". At first I did not think it was possible. I told myself that I was making a mistake. But on the way down the cliff he forgot his game for a moment and mentioned you as Clay – which he could not have known. And so all the questions I have been asking come up with the same answer ... You have been using me, flatfoot man. You and your friend use me. You did a great big thing of make-believe together.'

She relented for a moment and let him speak. 'Tony?' he started. 'What's got into you, Tony?'

'Goodbye,' she said. 'In spite of everything I hope

you escape the police. You know why? ... You never intend it, but you have been so very good to me.' She laughed. 'Don't be angry with your clumsy friend ... Over and out.'

She was far away when morning came; in another country. When she first opened her eyes in the hotel bedroom she couldn't for several long moments remember where she was; but everything soon jigsawed together. She felt under the pillow and pulled out what was there, staring with childlike wonder at the glittering brilliance of the Rivers diamond and the assortment of jewellery she had stuffed inside her rubber suit such an unreal time ago.

She was late down to breakfast, buying a newspaper from the stand on the way. An item with a Sardinia date-line in the second column leaped at her off the front page.

VILLA THIEVES' HAUL

Early this evening thieves broke into the Castello di Roccia, the Sardinian home of Mrs Barbara Ashley, and stole a number of items of jewellery from her bedroom at a time when Mrs Ashley was taking a bath ...

'Coffee?' a waiter interrupted.

... How the thieves entered the house is a mystery, since the grounds are extensively patrolled. However, despite the audacity of the theft, Mrs Ashley is not greatly concerned ...

'Coffee?'

... 'It was all imitation,' she stated. 'No one in her

right mind would leave the Rivers diamond just lying about. Or anything else of value for that matter. I have a special arrangement with the local bank whereby – irrespective of the hour – I am always able to call at the premises and visit the strongroom en route to wherever I happen to be going.'

'Coffee?' the waiter tried again.

Tears were rolling down Tony's cheeks; he hadn't noticed until now.

'I am sorry,' he apologised gravely. 'Is there anything I can do?'

She shook her head. To his surprise he realised she was laughing. In all his experience he had never seen such laughter. Baffled, he glanced at the newspaper.

'What is so funny?'

'Life,' he thought she said, but she was so convulsed by that time that it was impossible to be sure.

THE MISCHIEF DONE

by Edmund Crispin

'People are superstitious about diamonds,' said Detective Inspector Humbleby. 'They believe all sorts of extraordinary things. And of course diamonds do give us a lot of trouble at the Yard, one way and another.'

' "O Diamond! Diamond!" ' his host said.

'Is that a quotation? No, no, don't bother, leave it. Among the many delusions people have about diamonds —'

' "O Diamond! Diamond! Thou little knowest the mischief done!" ' Out of the depths of the armchair in his rooms in St Christopher's, Gervase Fen, University Professor of English Language and Literature, reached across with the decanter to pour more sherry into his guest's glass. 'Allegedly said by Isaac Newton,' he explained. 'His dog Diamond knocked over a candle and incinerated "the almost finished labours of some years".'

'Mathematicians oughtn't to keep dogs,' said Humbleby. 'And historians oughtn't to lend their manuscripts to John Stuart Mill.' He presumably meant Carlyle, part of whose *French Revolution* was used as kindling by Mill's housemaid. '*Rubies* are more valuable than diamonds,' Humbleby obstinately went on. 'And contrary to popular supposition, diamonds are very brittle. You can lose hundreds of pounds by just dropping one on a carpet.'

'Humbleby, what is all this about?'

And Humbleby, deflated, sighed. 'I've been made a fool of,' he said. 'Somebody went and stole an enormous great valuable diamond literally from under my nose, when I was supposed to be helping to protect it.'

'That's bad.'

'Not that the owner's lost it, mind.'

'That's good.'

'He's just hidden it somewhere, or rather, his brother has. The whole thing's an insurance fraud,' said Humbleby aggrievedly. 'We know it's that, but unfortunately we can't begin to prove it ... I don't enjoy being made a fool of.'

'No one does.'

'I should like somehow to get a bit of my own back.'

'Naturally, naturally.'

'So can you help me, do you think?'

'I very much doubt it,' said Fen. 'But tell me what happened, and I'll try.'

'The diamond's owner,' said Humbleby, 'was – and if I'm right about the business, still effectually is – a Soho jeweller called Asa Braham. Years ago he had a robbery, a genuine one, and I was put in charge of the investigation, and it went on for rather a long time, so I got to know Asa quite well. He's a wiry little man with frizzy black hair, fiftyish, very lively, very active; a charmer, and sharp-witted with it. I never exactly trusted him, but I did get to like him – and that was why I stupidly allowed myself to get involved in this business of the *Reine des Odalisques*.'

'Who on earth is she?'

'That's what the diamond's called. Its first owner, who christened it, was a Frenchman – apparently,' said Humbleby waspishly, 'a man of very little judgement, taste or even ordinary good sense. Anyway, it was from him that Asa Braham bought the thing, about six weeks ago now, for well over a hundred thousand pounds.'

'Good grief.'

'Yes, it was a lot, but although it was only mined quite recently it's become one of the famous diamonds. And Asa wanted it like mad, though he couldn't really afford it. You see, he's one of those jewellers who get obsessed with stones for their own sake – not at all a good thing from the commercial point of view (and in fact, Asa, though he's done adequately well, has never really flourished), but I suppose it has its satisfactions, even if I can't begin to imagine them myself. Asa passionately wanted that diamond; he *had* to have it; and he mortgaged himself to the hilt to pay the price. God alone knows what, apart from crime, he expected to do next. There he was with the *Reine*, doting on it, and nothing, psychologically, would have suited him better than to spend hours staring at the wretched bauble every day for the rest of his natural life. Yet if he'd actually settled down to that, he'd have been made bankrupt in a year or less. What I mean is that he just couldn't *afford* to keep the thing. Considered simply as a buy, the whole transaction was crazy: it isn't at all easy to dispose of hugely valuable stones even for what they cost, let alone at a profit; you may have to wait for years.'

'Fairly clear so far,' said Fen. 'You seem to have deviated, though. What about this earlier robbery? Genuine, you say?'

'Oh yes, definitely. We got the villains eventually, and put them away. Also, we got back some of the stones. On the rest, the insurance company paid – reluctantly.'

'Yes, they're always reluctant.'

'In this case, they were specially so. They didn't think Asa's precautions were good enough. But, God, jewellers,' said Humbleby with some feeling. 'I'll tell you what jewellers do: they roam about in dark alleys, at dead of night, with small fortunes rattling loose in their waistcoat pockets ... For the stones Asa didn't recover, as I said, the company paid. But the word went round that he was slack, and after that his insurance contracts were much stiffer, not just in terms of premiums but in terms of security too. So – he bought the *Reine*, and naturally he insured it, but there were a great many specific conditions. I've seen that contract – after the theft of the *Reine*, of course I was working in with the insurance company – and it's very tightly drawn indeed, as regards how the stone was looked after.

'So there you have it: the diamond bought about six weeks ago, and first carefully stowed away in the vault of Asa's shop, and then when four weeks ago Asa had to go off to Brazil on business, it was transferred to the safe deposit at Pratt's Bank in Portland Square.'

'Was that so very much safer, then?'

'The insurance company, Krafft International, certainly thought it was, at any rate for as long as Asa was out of the country. So Asa dutifully took it along there, with a Safeguard, the day before he left.'

'What safeguard?'

'Not what, who: a man from the Safeguard security corps. It was a condition of Asa's insurance contract that a Safeguard man had to be with the *Reine* whenever it wasn't actually under lock and key.'

Humbleby wriggled back into his chair and sipped his drink. 'So far, so good,' he presently went on. 'And what happened next was that a week ago Asa arrived back at London Docks on the *Luis Pizarro* – like me, he's terrified of aeroplanes, so he travelled both ways by sea – and rang me up the moment he got on shore, and asked me if I was free to come along with him and his precious diamond and the contractual Safeguard man on a trip to his cottage in Dorset, where he was scheduled to show the diamond off to a possible purchaser. Well, I didn't all that much want to go, but on the other hand the Yard's a terrible place nowadays, full of great grinning oafs who've never read a book for pleasure in their lives, and I get away from it whenever I possibly can. So here was an excuse of sorts, and I took it.'

'Yes, I can understand that all right,' said Fen. 'But what did he want you *for*? I mean, what did he *say*?'

'He said it'd be nice to see me again, and he was sure I'd like to have a look at the diamond.'

'And you believed that?'

'Well, not entirely,' said Humbleby. 'I thought there was probably something a bit funny going on. But that, you see, was all the more reason why I should be there. Only unfortunately, as it turned out, I wasn't quite suspicious enough. Anyway, I went.

'I went, and we met at Pratt's Bank. Asa came there direct from the docks – and by the way – there's absolutely no doubt about that: since the thing happened, we've checked and double-checked all of his movements, backwards, forwards and inside out, and he certainly had no time for any tricky business between getting off the boat and meeting me. I was the first to get to Pratt's. Then the Safeguard man arrived, a menacing figure called Shirtcliff. Last came Asa, full of the joys of spring. And I didn't like that. He was too cheerful altogether, for a man besotted with a diamond who's on the way to losing it to a customer after only a few weeks' ownership. He needed a customer, yes, and he was lucky to get one. Even so, he ought to have been just a bit glum about it, not completely cock-a-hoop.

'Asa went down into the vaults, and Shirtcliff and I went with him as far as the system allowed, which wasn't of course, the whole way. However, he was out again in a couple of minutes or less, waving a quite large black velvet jewel-box; and he handed this to Shirtcliff; and Shirtcliff took a look inside it, and grunted affirmatively, and shut the box up again, and put it in his brief-case; and we all went upstairs again, and out of the bank, and round the corner to where a self-drive hired car was waiting; and in that Asa drove us down to Stickwater in Dorset, me sitting beside him in the front passenger seat, and Shirtcliff in the back glowering and clutching his brief-case with the diamond in it.

'Our next consideration must be Asa's brother Ben.'

'Isn't this narrative becoming rather mannered, Humbleby?' said Fen restively. 'And by the way, is it going to turn out that there's some question of paste having been substituted for the real thing?'

'No, it isn't. That doesn't arise at all.'

'I see. Well, when is something going to happen?'

'In a moment, in a moment. Ben first. Ben is younger than his brother Asa, and much bigger and tougher. He's also the dependent one of the pair – did at one time have a jeweller's business of his own, but he was no good at it and it went bust. Since then he's lived off Asa, and also lived *with* Asa, either in their flat in London, or else in this dismal little house in Dorset. Ben looks after the domestic side, in so far as it gets looked after at all. They're neither of them married, and they do without servants, and they live together in a sort of devoted squalor.

'Envisage, then,' said Humbleby dramatically, 'this car – a puce Cortina, I ought perhaps to add – driving down from London to Stickwater in Dorset, Asa Braham at the wheel, myself beside him, the man Shirtcliff in the back, the diamond —'

'Humbleby, haven't you told me all this already?' Fen was more fretful than ever. 'And come to that, is something portentous or significant going to happen on this drive, something relevant, I mean, to what you seem to be trying to start out to describe to me?'

'Come to *that*,' said Humbleby a shade aggrievedly, 'aren't you being unduly particular? All I'm trying to do is give you the atmosphere, the ambient, the whole —'

'Yes, granted, and very nice too, but my point is that the drive itself —'

'It admittedly wasn't important.' Forced to this concession, Humbleby busied himself with finding and lighting a cheroot. 'Asa talked a good deal, but then, he always does, not just on drives, but on every occasion, everywhere. So at last, without incident, we arrived.'

'At last.'

'Not at any sort of gracious little country seat, but at a tiny, extraordinarily unprepossessing, example of Victorian farmhouse architecture, subsequently transformed, at no very evident expense, into a small dwelling-house. It was very isolated, with grounds which were, I suppose, fairly extensive, but horribly unkempt. As to the house itself, that really amounted to little more than two up, two down, with kitchen and bath: all dispiritingly grey and damp and obviously uncared-for. Ben Braham opened the front door for us, and seemed – I have to say "seemed" – in an evil temper. He took us into the front room right, a tattered sort of living-room, and offered us a drink. There was thereupon a row. The only drinks actually available, it turned out, were either home-brewed beer, made years before from some sort of chemist's kit, or a rather small amount of a dreadful Italian apéritif called Casca Oli. Ben was supposed to have got drink in, but for some reason (perhaps to give cogency to his being on bad terms with his brother Asa) hadn't in fact done so. He was supposed to have done a lot of things, including, in response to a radiogram from the *Luis Pizarro*, coming down earlier in the day to "open the house up". Well, he was there, all right, but that was about the most you could say. "I've packed my bag," he told us – and in fact there was a suitcase of some description hanging about in the hall outside – "and you know what I'm going to do? I m going to go back to London and have myself a bloody great piss-up."

'This announcement apparently didn't strike Asa favourably, giving rise, indeed, to a prolonged spell of angry fraternal shouting and counter-shouting. Even so, I stayed suspicious, as the words flew round and about my head. Meanwhile, the egregious Shirtcliff – who'd refused both Casca Oli and home-brewed beer, apparently more on principle than because they were equally odious – continued to nurse the *Reine des Odalisques* in its fat jewel-box in his brief-case on his lap.

'So there we all four of us were, in this awful living-room, sipping ullage while a row went on. And now, to make a fifth, the potential customer for the *Reine* arrived. You've heard of Clyde Savitt?'

'The film star.'

'Yes.'

'He buys diamonds for his wife.'

'Yes : like Richard Burton – though perhaps on not

quite so massive a scale.'

'And he's an expert on diamonds, isn't he?'

'Yes – again like Burton, I suppose, up to a point. But with Savitt there's an extra dimension. Savitt *père* was a jeweller, and Savitt *fils*, before he went into pictures, was intended to become one too. So before the lures of the old *ciné* trapped him, he learned a lot, about diamonds particularly. In short, he'd be pretty nearly impossible to deceive. He wanted the *Reine* for his wife; he knew it, from its many photographs; and when he eventually *saw* it ...'

Humbleby sucked at his cheroot, long and deep. 'We went,' he said, 'into the room on the other side of the little hallway. That is, all of us did except Ben, who was still – and again I have to say "apparently" – sulking. Savitt, I gathered, was resting between pictures at a modest country house conveniently close by. He had come to Asa, rather than the other way round, because he didn't want his wife to know anything at all in advance about this possible jewel-transaction. It was all perfectly plausible, and perfectly plain.

'What was less plausible, and certainly less immediately plain, was why we'd made the move from the one room to the other at all. (I can see the reasons now, of course, but then, hindsight's a wonderful thing.) Asa's notion was that in the living-room where we'd all started off, Savitt included, the light wasn't adequate, or at any rate, not adequate for examining a diamond. But this deficiency, though certainly real enough, didn't seem to be much remedied when we got to Asa's "study", which had in its ceiling a bulb of very low wattage indeed, so much so that although it was a small room, and we were crowded together, we could barely make out the expressions on each other's faces ... I must now,' said Humbleby with some dignity, 'describe this room to you.'

'Yes, yes, of course.'

'Small, then. And not what you'd call over-furnished, either. There was a round table, at about the middle. There was a minute flat-topped desk with nothing on it. There was an almost equally exiguous old-fashioned safe – completely empty, it subsequently transpired. There were a crack-springed armchair, and a desk chair. And finally, in one corner, you could see a huddle of old Casca Oli cartons, with a couple of Anglepoise lamps and a few other odd bits and pieces. No pictures, and only one window, and that had steel shutters over it, closed and locked. By way of making light conversation, Asa explained that they'd been closed and locked for years, he having lost the only key. The shutters had been put in, he said, at a time when he'd been in the habit of bringing stones down to Stickwater, until finally the insurance companies had said, to his great grief, that he mustn't do it any longer. Also from earlier, less stringent days dated the safe, and the admittedly pretty solid door – much more solid, as we found to our cost, than any of the others in the house – which we'd come in by.

'Light, Asa said: we must have, he said, like the dying Goethe, more light; and he started fussing with the two Anglepoises, neither of which, it soon became clear, was fitted with a plug in any way corresponding with the one socket in the room's skirting-board. (By now, I need hardly tell you, my suspicions were very serious indeed. But even so, how was *I* to know what was planned, what was in fact just about to happen?) Anyway, there it was: Asa fatuously muttering about adaptors, Ben presumably still in the living-room (or possibly already off, with his prepared suitcase, for his

projected piss-up in London); Clyde Savitt, the unlucky Shirtcliff and my almost equally unlucky self
hovering around Asa in this dreadful little room, waiting for inchoate possibilities to congeal into some sort
of event. This they almost immediately did, but not
before Clyde Savitt, tiring like the rest of us of Asa's
busy fumblings with flexes, suggested that we might
perfectly well have a preliminary look at the *Reine*
straightaway. And Asa was all for this. Leaving the
Anglepoises, he gave instructions to Shirtcliff. And
with the air of a man acting insufferably against his
better judgement, Shirtcliff took the jewel-box from
his brief-case, placed it in the middle of the round table
and retired angrily to stand with his back against the
super-special door, which we'd closed after us. Shirtcliff had already inspected, and found sound, the steel
window-shutters; now he was adopting what even a
much more intelligent man would of course have
thought the best general defensive position available.

'He was wrong about that, but really, one can
scarcely blame him.

'Jewel-box on table, then; and Asa advances on it,
opens it reverently and stands gazing at its contents,
even under that impossibly dim illumination, with the
pride of a Mrs Worthington whose daughter has not
only gone on the stage, but unaccountably made a spectacular success of the business. As to Clyde Savitt,
whose behaviour up to this point had been impeccable,
excitement overcame him. He snatched the *Reine* out
of the box (Shirtcliff stiffening visibly), snatched a
loupe from his pocket and stood there making his
examination in a breathless silence which affected all
of us.

'Then he said, "Yes: that's it, all right." '

'I mention this crucial remark not to criticise its

civility, nor even to suggest that diamond-mad people
go diamond-mad whenever they see a diamond, to the
exclusion of absolutely everything else. I mention it
because it was *true*. You said something earlier about
the possibility of paste. But Savitt was sure then, and is
sure now, that what he had in his hand was the *Reine*
and nothing but the *Reine* – and this in spite of the
awful light and the unfortunate circumstances generally.

'Savitt said, "Yes: that's it, all right. And I want to
buy it." And he put it back in its box, rather quickly, as
if it was burning his fingers.

'And then suddenly we were in complete darkness.'

Humbleby shook his head, not in negation but sadly.
An efficient officer, he was consequently finding his
own part in these proceedings disagreeable to recall.

'Looking back on it,' he said, 'I remember, or imagine I remember, the click of the mains switch. This,
along with the meter and so forth, was in the hallway
immediately outside the study. And it was this, certainly, that was used. So there we were, in chaos and
old night, with the little gleam of the diamond in its
open jewel-box on the round table our only illumination of any sort. By then it was blackness outside the
house – no moon or stars; and even if it hadn't been,
the steel shutters over the window would have cut out
any light absolutely.

'Then the door burst open (no light at all from the
hallway outside), and someone came tearing into the
room, and the gleam of the diamond winked out, and
the someone ran off again, and the door slammed, shutting us in; and the footsteps went away, out of the front
door, and crunched quickly along the drive out of ear-

shot; and somewhere distantly, a car engine started and revved up, and then that was gone too.

'From the moment of the light going out to the moment of the intruder nipping off again, and slamming the door, was, I suppose, scarcely more than three seconds. Enough, though, for the *Reine* to be gone.

'Shirtcliff had been bashed in the small of the back by the door opening, and had gone sprawling. Even so, he was the first to recover. But it was hopeless. Thanks to Asa's precautions, the room door had a Yale on it; and the intruder had reversed the snib as he rushed in; so all he had to do when he left was click the door shut and reverse the snib on the outer side (there exist, unfortunately, Yales with this double arrangement).

'And we were trapped.'

Again shaking his head, 'We were trapped,' said Humbleby, 'for close on two hours. I know this must seem nearly incredible, but you must remember those shutters, and also the fact that there was no telephone, and also the fact that apart from my cigarette-lighter, which was by no means inexhaustible, we couldn't see a bloody thing we were doing. Of course we shouted, and we banged. But Ben, it appeared, the only other person in the house, had long since left, plus suitcase, for his mafficking in London. That, anyway, was his story, when it came to the crunch : he'd gone off almost straightaway after we moved from the living room to the study. And this never was, nor could be, disproved. Me, I never believed it for a moment. I was as sure as could be that it was Ben who'd turned off the mains switch, careered into the room, nabbed the diamond and whisked off out again, all with the happy collaboration of his brother Asa. But proving that was, and is, something else again. Shirtcliff could have had an accomplice, or even, come to that, Clyde Savitt. What, at that stage, did we know? What *could* we know?

'I'm fairly good at locks, but there were no tools – apart from scraps of Anglepoises which Shirtcliff tore apart with his bare hands – so as I've said, it was nearly two hours before we got that door open at last. Hanging on to Shirtcliff's sleeve, with the lighter guttering in my hand, I hauled him outside, turned the mains switch back on and then hauled him back inside again.

' "Strip!" I said.

'To do him justice, he saw the point, and he stripped at once. I went over his discarded clothes very carefully, and then, equally carefully, I went over *him*. (We're supposed, at the Yard, to have read a lot of books about such things, and I can distinctly remember glancing through one or two of the least offensive of them.) Asa, who was putting on a great act of shock and horror, at this stage started bellowing about bodily orifices, but as I pointed out to him, not just the diamond had disappeared from the study, but a bloody great jewel-case as well. Bodily orifices, I pointed out to Asa, were very unlikely receptacles for that. And in fact the jewel-case was eventually found, thrown away at the side of the drive, only a few yards from the front door. By that time, it was, I need hardly say, empty.

'Shirtcliff – "clean" – ran off to a telephone with instructions from me. Meanwhile, I myself went over the study with what writers inexperienced in hyphenation call a fine tooth-comb, and which —'

'Humbleby, listen a moment. It —'

'– and which, I can assure you, brought nothing whatever, of any relevance, to light. I also searched Savitt and Asa, and they searched me. Still nothing. And there could be nothing. Someone had burst in, and grabbed the *Reine* in its box, and disappeared again, and that was all there was to it. Still, I *had* to take all the precautions, I *had* to do the searching – just in case. But nothing. I was very scrupulous about it all, and I can assure you – nothing, then or afterwards.'

Fen stared at his guest with more than usual attention: he had found the tale, if not exactly brilliant, at any rate an interesting one. 'And finally?' he prompted.

'Finally, Ben Braham was stopped in his car by the police at Deare, getting on for eighty miles from Stickwater, two-and-a-half hours' drive. No diamond on him or in him, of course, and no diamond anywhere in the car. How could there have been? Eighty miles! At any point, at his leisure, knowing perfectly well how appallingly we were trapped back at that loathsome little house, he could have turned off the London road into a lane, stopped at a field-gate, gone into the field, poked a hole with his finger in the bank, injected the diamond, covered it up, made a careful note of the place (he had a torch in his car, but that doesn't prove anyone guilty of anything) and then simply traipsed back and driven on again. He could, and can, simply return and pick the miserable little object up again whenever it suits him.'

'Which won't be yet.'

'No, of course not yet: probably not for a long time. Not, anyway, until a long time after Krafft has paid out the insurance money. Ben and Asa will know, in any case, that we shall be keeping an eye on them for a bit. They won't make any move until they're completely certain it won't backfire in the form of a Conspiracy to Defraud charge.'

'And when they do at last make their move to pick up the diamond,' said Fen: 'what then? Does Asa Braham get it anonymously through the post from a conscience-stricken thief?'

'Lord, no.' And Humbleby smiled, with some affection, at his host, whom it was pleasing to find, for the moment, almost as dim-witted as he, Humbleby, had throughout the whole Braham business felt himself to be. 'Because in that case, you see, the insurance money would have to be repaid, and Asa wouldn't be able to afford that. But it'll be reward enough, for Asa, just to have the *Reine* back and be able to gloat over it secretly. As I've told you, he's crazy about stones. And that, I suppose, has been the basis of the whole trouble.'

Fen thought for a bit. Then he said mildly, 'Superstitions about diamonds. You started by talking about those – but you don't, if I may say so, seem to be altogether free from them yourself.'

'I know practically everything about diamonds,' said Humbleby, with some indignation. 'Diamonds, now —'

'Yes, of course. But you say that when the lights went out – and there was no sort of reflected light – this particular diamond shone in the dark.'

'Yes, certainly it did. Diamonds are self-luminescent. Look up any book on the subject and you'll find —'

'No, I shan't. Sorry, Humbleby, but not for the circumstances *you've* described. Diamonds do shine in the dark, yes. But they don't produce light, like glowworms. They store it and reproduce it. For a diamond to shine in the dark, it must have been subjected to light first – fairly bright light, and fairly recently.

'But what sort of light had your precious *Reine des Odalisques* been under? Well, if the tales are true, it'd been for three weeks in the darkness of a bank's safe-deposit vault; then a man called Shirtcliff glanced at it for a moment, in ordinary daylight; finally, it was exposed to a low-wattage bulb for what doesn't sound like much more than two minutes, though I suppose —'

'*Less* than two minutes.' Humbleby struck his brow, with his clenched fist, in a transpontine manner which was nevertheless patently sincere. 'God, what an imbecile I've been! You mean, Asa was so infatuated with the thing that he took it with him to South America.'

'Yes, that seems likely.'

'And then marched into Pratt's Bank with it in his pocket, and then simply popped it into the jewel-box which he *had* left there, and brought it out again.'

'Almost certain, I'd say. The diamond had stored all that light because he was staring at it virtually up to the last possible moment. Either he'd forgotten that when Ben put their plan into operation the diamond would shine, or else – which seems more likely – he just thought that the interval, between the light going out and the *Reine* being grabbed, would be too short for anyone to notice.'

'Well, *I* noticed,' said Humbleby. 'The question is, did Savitt? Did Shirtcliff? If they both did' – and here an unhealthy revengeful gleam appeared in Humbleby's eye – 'Asa's claim on Krafft Insurance isn't going to look too good.'

'If he disgracefully neglected a specified precaution, then the whole thing is void.'

'Void.'

'And did only Asa have access to that Pratt's Bank safe-deposit? I mean, if he could just give the key to someone else, then he could say —'

'No, it had to be him. Couldn't be anyone else.'

And here Fen considered Humbleby with a faint air of displeasure which, except between such old friends, might have seemed slightly ungracious. 'I don't altogether dislike the sound of your Asa,' he said. 'Of course, it's bad to try and defraud insurance companies, and if for all of you that diamond did in fact shine in the dark, then ... Even so, there are some moods' – and here, Fen brought the sherry out again – 'in which it's possible to feel that the thing was worth a try.'

'Asa withdrew his claim,' said Humbleby when six months later he and Fen met coincidentally at the Travellers', 'because Savitt and Shirtcliff had both, like me, glimpsed the *Reine* self-luminescing. So the claim wouldn't wash – and now, I understand, Asa's quite a poor man. He makes out, though, as poor men so often mysteriously do. Is your conscience at rest?'

'Shirtcliff?'

'Sacked from Safeguard for incompetence, and at once taken on by the Metropolitan Police.'

'Savitt?'

'Richer and more famous and more courteous than ever.'

'The diamond?'

'Well ... Somewhere. I suppose we'll never know.'

They never did know, but at the last, one man, without knowing it, knew.

Police Constable Bowker's 'manor' was centred on the hamlet of Amble Harrowby, a focus for much rich agricultural activity. Left-wing himself, Bowker was unable to suppress at least a theoretical distaste for the local Socialist peer, Lord Levin, whose notional egalitarianism had somehow never prevented him from enjoying such benefits as an inherited title, with additional tremendous inherited wealth, could bestow.

At the same time, Bowker realised that in this respect he was perhaps being a little naive, the more so as Lord Levin went to such particular trouble to be pleasant to everyone, Bowker himself by no means excluded. There could scarcely – Bowker reflected, as he buzzed through the lanes in his white crash-helmet, on his little machine – be a more agreeably conscienceless man in the entire land.

In particular, this scheme of a trout-lake was good. Lord Levin had many farm tenancies on his property; one of these – always notable for the combined age, idleness and incapacity of its tenant – had recently been caused to be vacated by death; and Lord Levin was taking the opportunity of converting some fifteen acres of notoriously unproductive land into a fairly large-scale water for fishing.

Now, Police Constable Bowker, whatever his general feelings about Lord Levin, didn't at all disapprove of this. On the contrary, since the lake was to be a natural-seeming sort, confluent with the surrounding mild bulges of the countryside, he felt, and felt quite strongly, that here was an instance where private riches might quite well redound to the public good.

He stopped his machine, therefore, at a specially good point of vantage – Copeman's Rise – from which the lake-making proceedings, which had by now been going on for a good two weeks, could be unusually well viewed.

Immense scars, bulldozer-induced, lay across the land. Hedgerows had been ripped up and tossed aside. Tons of unsifted earth were being lorry-laden and whipped off to unknown dumping-grounds. The whole spectacle – admittedly for the moment hideous, but still, Bowker felt, marginally better than the grubby little contraceptive-infested copses it was replacing –

was one of massive alteration and change. Bowker's heart warmed. Soon, all this unavoidable scooping-out would give way to a placid expanse of brownish waters (Bowker's romanticism would have preferred bluish, but his practicality forbade this), lightly ruffled by the prevailing winds.

So far, so good. But as Bowker came to a halt, it became evident to him that his emotions regarding this presently tormented landscape, so soon to be converted to beauty, were not entirely shared. Two men, who had parked their shabby car close by, were having to support each other, arms round shoulders, in order to contemplate the scene with equanimity.

Bowker thought that he perhaps recognised them. They were a jeweller and his brother with a country cottage at Stickwater, fifteen miles away. Bowker also thought that they were possibly supporting one another because they were drunk.

But then he shifted a little nearer – and decided he had been wrong about that.

Bowker went back to his machine, re-started the engine, gunned it up and headed for the London road. There are some things even a country copper thinks it best not to interfere with : and one is when he sees two male adults watching a trout-lake being made with great scalding tears pouring down their cheeks.

JUNO'S SWANS

by Celia Dale

So: the last of England. But I am not one of Mr Ford Madox Brown's hollow-eyed consumptives, nor do I have some pallid virgin clinging to my arm, the very picture of wan defeat. Leaning on the rail of this P and O steamship, I confess to a singular satisfaction as I watched the murky shores of my homeland recede. I have done with her, with everything that held me there. I have no ties. I shall occupy my time on shipboard very tolerably. No doubt there will be whist; I shall make my regular perambulations round the deck morning and afternoon; I shall, if requested, contribute a dramatic monologue to the ship's concert; I shall devote my civilities to mature ladies travelling under the protection of their husbands and to young ladies travelling under that of their mamas. A man of intelligence – and I flatter myself I am far from being a fool – will hardly put his head into the same noose twice.

So here I am, ensconced in the solitude of the Writing Room, feeling the ship begin its slow plunge and rise as we move into open water, hearing the footsteps and voices of the other passengers as they bustle up and down the passageways, exploring the mighty monster that will be their home and haven for so many weeks before we reach Bombay. In an hour or two the dinner bell with sound. Until then it amuses me to sit here undisturbed and to commit to the thick sheets of steamship notepaper, handsomely embossed with pennants and anchors, the singular events which led me to leave my native shores. England, farewell! To paraphrase Cardinal Wolsey, Farewell, a long farewell to all my weakness!

I first met Emmeline at the house of mutual friends in Portman Square. It was a musical evening and I had been prevailed upon, after the tenors and sopranos had been heard, to give my rendering of Mr Irving's famous soliloquy from 'The Bells'. I confess I do it well – I was a leading light in my University theatricals, and no doubt it was my historic bent which led me to read for the Bar, although happily I have never been required to earn my living from it. The Bar or the pulpit are the only alternatives to a gentleman with a talent for drama, and I had no taste for the pulpit.

When my recitation ended I was surrounded by a host of cooing ladies: So powerful, so tragic, so thrilling, quite blood-curdling! And when the tide of lace, ribbons and flounces had receded I found my hand encased by the small kid-gloved fingers of a girl, fair and pale as a fairy, small as an elf, who stared up at me with great violet eyes. 'You will haunt my dreams,' she said in a sighing sort of voice.

An elderly gent, fat and purple of jowl, thrust up behind her. 'Capital, capital! Better than the Lyceum, I assure you!'

'You're too kind,' I said, or something of the sort.

'Not a bit of it, sir. Capital, quite striking!'

The young lady had released my hand and stood now with downcast eyes, playing with her fan.

'I trust I shall not seriously disturb this young lady's dreams,' I said. 'I have no desire to be a bogeyman.'

'What? Bogeyman? Nonsense, sir, nonsense! Too fanciful, Emmeline – my daughter, sir, and I am Colonel ...' well, it doesn't matter who. Within six months he was dead, struck down by an apoplexy, which was not surprising considering his size and the amount of brandy he poured into himself. A decent old codger, though, who took me to his heart for dual reasons: firstly, he had no son and, like all military men, regretted it. Although I am far from being the kind of fellow such a man might be thought to have admired (for I abhor your bluff, hard-drinking Service type whose only talk is whores and horses) I was in fact, I surmise, what he would secretly have liked as a son. I am tall, elegant, handsome – no need for false modesty here. I do not bluster or guffaw, my control is perfect yet my histrionic talent shows that I am capable of feeling.

His second reason, without doubt, was the desire to see his daughter safely married and to someone in whom he had perfect confidence. She was something of an heiress; but that, he soon found out, was immaterial to me, since I have ample means of my own. She was also delicate; her mother had died a few years after her birth (which had no doubt accelerated an inevitable decline) and Emmeline had inherited a constitutional weakness which made her frail as a flower and sometimes as beautiful. Her father, good old man, was anxious that she should not wed some coarse-grained fellow who would wear her out with child-bearing but someone who would cherish and encourage her frail energies and bring her the tranquillity she needed.

Such a man was myself. I am not a sensual man. I won't deny that I have, from time to time in my youth, patronised the better houses of Mayfair or kept a dollymop for a month or two in some discreet Kennington villa; but the gross beauties of the Haymarket were not for me, I have ever been far too fastidious, too elevated in spirit to wallow, as my fellow students did, in the stews and taverns of the metropolis.

There was something about Emmeline to which this

delicacy in my nature responded. She was small and
frail as a fairy, with fair hair that curled and fronded
over her white brow and those great violet eyes. Her
skin was pale and gauzy, like the wings one almost
thought to see at her shoulders as, when she was in
health, she flitted here and there about the house and
grounds of ... let us call it Haylett Hall. She was like
some fragile flower that too easily wilts and fades, but,
like them, she could revive and bloom again after some
days of rest, her light, breathless voice trilling once
more through the panelled rooms and passages of the
house.

She aroused in me a singular mixture of emotions:
a masculine instinct to protect and dominate, a curiosity as to the essence of her charm, something of a
collector's pleasure in a rare and delicate piece, the
pleasure of possession. Her white and childlike beauty
attracted me strongly.

I had asked the Colonel for her hand two months
after our meeting. He had embraced me, the engagement was announced, the wedding date arranged, and
then he died. Amidst our tears we decided to continue
as had been planned, for it was what he would have
wished and the wedding was in any event to be a quiet
one in the village church close by the Hall.

Thus it was. A brief honeymoon at Broadstairs (we
did not venture abroad, for Emmeline dreaded the
sea) and we returned to Haylett Hall to start our new
life together – as had been planned from the beginning,
for we would have lived as son and daughter with the
Colonel, had he been spared.

Haylett Hall is not large but it is commodious and it
is beautiful. Built in the reign of Charles the Second,
it has undergone various additions and enrichments,
mainly in the time of George the Fourth. It has been

in Emmeline's family for some two hundred years and the gardens, parkland and the strange wild area known as the Workings have been enlarged and beautified over that period. It was a property to be proud of and I was proud of it – indeed, it is perhaps the only single thing that I regret leaving behind me.

We settled in. It seemed a perfect life. I did not regret relinquishing my barrister's chambers, since I had hardly practised. We had an ample circle of acquaintances within the neighbourhood, a well-trained staff of servants – and Sybil.

Sybil. I confess I have paused in my narrative a while after writing that name. Sybil. As dark as Emmeline was fair, almost as tall as I, slender and swift as a sword. Sybil.

Of course I had known about Sybil. I had met her whenever I visited Haylett Hall to pay my addresses to Emmeline, and had escorted the two of them on their calls about the county. The two girls had been friends from childhood, had grown up together under the Colonel's care when Sybil's parents were tragically murdered by tribesmen near Kabul – the two men were brother officers and friends. It was Sybil who ran the household, who cared for Emmeline when she was ill, who nursed the old man through his final days. Something between an elder sister and a companion, she was as much a part of the house, I soon came to understand, as the panelling itself or the dark portraits on the stairs; and like them she did not obtrude herself, but seemed to be always there should she be needed, discreetly absent so that Emmeline and I could be alone during our courtship, present again for a hand of whist, a tramp over the countryside, an evening's laughter and song round the piano in the large, log-lit drawing room. As strong as Emmeline was weak, she was an ever-present part of life at Haylett Hall, watchful for our comfort, a smile ever hovering on her lips, her dark eyes ever alert.

When the old man had died, and Emmeline lay prostrate in her room, tear-stained and weak with grief, Sybil had come to me as I sat before the fire in the library, musing on the enigma of mortality. Her eyes were red but there was no weakness in her manner. Direct as always, she said, 'Lewis,' she said, 'I hope you will not postpone the wedding.'

I murmured that I had not so intended.

'I'm glad,' she said, clasping her long hands nervously so that the chatelaine she wore at her belt swung and tinkled against her skirt. 'It will be best for Emmeline. With the Colonel gone, she may so easily decline. She needs a man's authority to order her affairs, to hold her grasp on life. My care for her is not enough.'

'I swear solemnly that mine shall be.'

'Yes.' She looked at me, direct and dark. 'Yes, that is what I believe. It is for her sake, you see. It is what is best for her.' She turned and left the room. We never spoke of it again.

So we were man and wife, Emmeline and I. My flower, my fairy was mine, we talked and ate, played music and cards together, walked a little if the weather were fine, not too far and not too fast, drove out in the carriage, well wrapped up with rugs, went to London for a few weeks in the season if she were up to it, leaving Sybil at home. We shared a life together, Emmeline and I; but it was not a married life.

I need not be too delicate. Who, after all, will read this tale but I? That fairy, that gossamer girl who had so entranced and intrigued my senses, was no more a woman than is a whiting upon the fishmonger's slab.

I am not, as I have said, a sensual man. I can forgo the pleasures of the flesh without inconvenience if circumstances order it. But marriage postulates certain activities, certain rights, and these not only was my poor Emmeline quite ignorant of but cringed from when the facts were known.

For some months I persevered, but although I conquered her resistance I never overcame her horror of this natural act – no doubt her terror of childbirth played some part in this, one must be charitable. Whatever the causes, connubial life with Emmeline soon became at first a mockery, then a penance, finally nothing. I moved out of the matrimonial bedroom into a handsome room the other side of the house, drawing on all my resources of fortitude and self-sufficiency to build a tolerable life of my own, as indifferent as I could make myself to the twittering, childish ninny I had somehow married and who was rapidly (due, no doubt, to the lengthening periods spent bed-ridden or lying upon sofas in a perhaps unconscious retreat from her obligations) growing fat.

I will not dwell upon that period of my life. Schooled in self-discipline though I am, even now I can scarce control the bitter anger, the resentment of those days, denied the comforts to which I had the right, including that of children. All men desire a son. I won't pretend I care much for children, with their squalls and squabbles (I trust there aren't too many aboard this ship) but I had the right to expect my name, my talents and my handsome figure to be perpetuated. Well, no matter ...

I lived sufficient to myself, affable to my neighbours, courteous to my wife, cold behind a mask of polite indifference. But slowly, more and more – Sybil.

My eyes were drawn to her when she was present, my

thoughts when she was absent. Slowly she possessed first my waking reveries, then my dreams – dreams such as I had never experienced before. In them she was half naked, her slender body maddeningly revealed through torn or opened garments, shameless, lewd ... In my dreams she spoke words from the gutter, made gestures from the stews. She drew me on, shuddering, wild ... and in the morning I would look at her, neat and bright in her sensible country clothes, pouring the coffee, passing the kedgeree, adjusting Emmeline's rug, putting the slippers on those useless feet, holding the cup while she drank, gently brushing back that frizzing hair – and my eyes would burn at her over that mockery and she would meet my gaze, direct, bright, then turn aside to tend yet further the soft pale slug our fairy had become.

Sometimes, if Emmeline were well enough to come downstairs, I would find Sybil's gaze fixed upon me over the couch where my wife lay. Sometimes our hands would touch, she withdrawing hers with a swift movement and averted eyes. She kept more and more to Emmeline's rooms, but when we encountered one another her eyes sought mine again, dark, burning, questing. Once, when the doctor had just taken his leave after Emmeline had suffered one of her collapses, we stood at the foot of the stairs together, she almost as tall as I, her pale red-mouthed face lamp-lit, her eyes brilliant. She laid a hand on my arm and said, her voice trembling, 'She is suffering, Lewis.'

I covered her hand with mine and dared to say, 'We are all suffering here.'

'Yes. Yes, that's true.' She withdrew her hand, glancing nervously at the parlourmaid who passed down the hall after seeing the doctor out. So low I could hardly hear her, she said, 'I can't bear to see her suffer.'

She turned and went swiftly up the stairs, back to Emmeline's side, holding her long skirts in one delicate hand, the white neck bent under the dark knot of hair that in my dreams had been so wild, so tangled. Watching her go, I said in my heart, You shall not, dearest. We will suffer no more.

I don't propose to go in detail into what followed. The practicalities are tedious and unimportant. Suffice it to say that it is uncommonly easy to obtain arsenic in sufficient quantities to kill an army, if you declare it is an army of rats, that no name I ever gave any chemist astute enough to desire one was ever verified, and that if one's purchases are made sufficiently far afield there is singularly little chance that anyone will ever recognise one. Add to all this a trusting domestic staff, a show of concern and husbandly attention, patience and common sense, and you will readily understand how Emmeline's illness, slight at first following that collapse, increased to a distressing and ultimately fatal conclusion. She was only twenty-eight.

Sybil was prostrated. We all were. The maids crept about red-eyed and snivelling, the butler and my own man looked grave as undertakers, the neighbours called dripping crape and condolences. I kept to my room for twenty-four hours, for truth to tell the event had taken its toll of me. When I issued forth again I was astonished at my haggard appearance, pale and distinguished like the Commendatore in *Don Juan*. I went about the sad business attendant upon death, mourned with the doctor over madeira and biscuits in the darkened library, accepted his regrets that medical skill, alas ... and was afire for Sybil. Her maid told me she was prostrated still. The doctor prescribed sleeping draughts. I paced the silent house and empty gardens, wild with impatience to see that lovely form appear, haggard and tear-stained though she needs must be, sad too at the passing of a childhood friend, but looking at me with that clear bright gaze, the dark hair burning from the high brow, the slender figure vibrant ...

Behind my grave composure I was mad with longing. My dreams mingled with my yearning till I felt I must rush and beat upon her door, throw myself in upon her, on her ... I held myself rigid, schooled and disciplined to the outside world, a flawless performance. I sat, I waited; I walked, and waited. At last she came.

It was at the Workings, that strange wilderness of wood and quarry, of tangled bushes and treacherous paths where they say ancient Britons delved for flint, thick with trees and undergrowth now down its steep sides, with the glimpse of stagnant water at the bottom where once men had hacked at the rock. There is a path along the top, heavy with blackberries and fox-gloves in their season, and at its curve a wooden seat, for the prospect opens out just there and you can see across the quarry to the hills beyond the village, the far side of the valley. It was the afternoon before the funeral and I had fled the house and my intolerable waiting, had taken a walking-stick and slashed my way through the wood to the Workings path and the bench, and there Sybil was sitting. She was weeping, her head in its simple bonnet bent into her hands, the veil thrown back. She started to her feet as I appeared.

'Lewis!'

'My dearest!' It burst from me in a groan and I held out my arms to her. She came into them like a bird, quivering and sobbing. I felt her slender body against mine, strong and smooth and so wonderfully alive. I took the bonnet gently from her head and dropped it on the bench, smoothed the hair from her wet cheeks. 'Sybil,' I said, 'Sybil ...'

'Oh Lewis . . .' She lifted her head and looked at me, eyes drenched in tears. 'Oh Lewis, what shall I do? How can I bear it?'

'Hush, my dearest, we will bear it together. It is my burden rather than yours.'

'No, no, it is mine.' She pushed herself free and took a few steps away. 'You don't know – you can't know. What can my life be now?'

I stepped forward and took her hand. 'Your life will be with me, Sybil. In a little while, when a decent interval has passed. With me, Sybil, with me . . .' I covered her hand with kisses.

'What?' She stared at me and stepped backwards, pulling her hand away. 'What are you saying?'

'That I love you, Sybil. I have longed to say it for months, years, to shout it aloud, to breathe it in your ears. I have longed to say it with my lips, to hear you say it with yours rather than with your eyes, your burning, brilliant eyes . . .'

'You are mad!' she cried.

'With love, with longing! Sybil . . .' I seized her hand again, striving to draw her to me once more and kiss at last that red, red mouth.

With violent strength she thrust me from her. 'You are mad!' she repeated. 'Mad! What fantasy is this?'

'No fantasy but a dream dreamed by us both. I saw it in your voice, your eyes. While she lived we were mute, but now . . . My dearest, my only passionate love . . .'

With all her strength she struck me across the face. She was breathing fast, her eyes wildly blazing, her voice shrill. 'You fool!' she cried. 'You mad, evil fool! I never loved you, I could never love you! It was she I loved, she, she, my silver flower, my gentle, tender woman – only she, only she ...' She began to weep again.

I stared at her. 'You loved my wife?'

'Yes, yes, always! It was only she ...'

'You loved her – as I love you?'

'More, much more. What can men know of love ...'

I struck her. She was near the edge, and she fell. After a while the bushes were silent again, the stagnant water still. I threw her bonnet after her.

Well, that's how it was. I returned to the house. Eventually there was a hue and cry. Eventually she was found. By the time the search party had trampled the path there was a plethora of footprints. And fortunately the marks where she had struck my cheek were hidden by my beard.

It was not quite possible to hold a double funeral; and I saw to it that they lay in different parts of the churchyard. No one else should lie down with what I had thought to be my Sybil. I saw to it that, unlike Juno's swans, they should not any longer be coupled and inseparable.

Ah, there's the dinner bell. This narrative is nicely timed. It has done me good to write it – confession is good for the soul, they say, but I have been more concerned to lay the facts on paper as a study into the singularly odd delusions that can ensnare the human heart. I must, as Sybil said, have been mad.

I am not mad now. I am extremely in possession of myself and ever shall be. I shall make my way to the stern of this vessel, drop this narrative page by page into its creaming wake, then go below to the Saloon and have my dinner. The first night out to sea one does not dress.

THE LONG WAY ROUND

by Elizabeth Ferrars

Leo woke with a headache, and even before he had
opened his eyes to the hard stripes of light that fell
across his bed through the slats of the Venetian blinds,
he knew that it was going to be one of his bad ones.
There was the familiar band of pain above his eyebrows. There was the feeling of nausea. Soon it would
be far worse. Daylight would became unbearable. He
would probably be sick.

With a groan, he sat up, wondering where Melanie
had put the codeine tablets.

Swinging his feet down on to the cool tiled floor, he
sat on the edge of the bed, a lean, narrow-shouldered
man who because of his baldness looked more than the
forty-nine years that he was. Holding his head in his
hands, he fought off the dizziness that made the room
swim and the dark dots before his eyes glide about like
tadpoles in a tank. Then he got up carefully and crossed
to the corner where the suitcases were.

Both of them were open, but had been no more than
half-unpacked. The evening before, when he and
Melanie had reached the hotel, they had both been so
tired that they had only grabbed at the few things that
they had needed for the night, had drunk the double
whiskies that they had had sent up to their room and
had fallen into bed. The journey had taken about twice
as long as it should have. There had been a two hour
delay at Heathrow, another almost as long at Athens,
then there had been difficulty about finding a taxi to
take them to their hotel in Nicosia. Frustration and ten-

sion had had time to build up in Leo, enough to account for the headache this morning. Unless, of course, it came from plain fear. Yet he was not aware of feeling frightened.

From the other bed Melanie said, 'What are you doing?'

'I want the codeine,' Leo said. 'I've got a headache.'

'It's the heat,' she said in a husky, half-awake voice. 'You aren't used to it, that's the trouble.'

He was pawing about in the nearer of the two suit-cases, the one that had most of his own clothes in it.

'Damn it, where did you put the stuff?' he asked.

But as he said it, his groping hand touched something in the suitcase and he froze in horror, such horror that for the moment he forgot his headache. The gun. The gun buried in a handful of socks. The gun that nobody knew he had, not even Melanie. Particularly not Melanie.

But how in the world had he managed to be such a fool as to leave it in the open suitcase all night, where Melanie, perhaps wakeful in the unfamiliar heat and looking for a book to pass the time with, might have found the thing while he himself slept deeply and unguardedly? Was it an omen, a sort of warning, that there was something wrong with his plan?

'Not in there,' Melanie said. 'In the zip-bag.'

She got out of bed and came padding across the room towards him, her body formless inside her loose, pink-flowered, cotton nightgown. Her grey-streaked hair hung in limp strands about her bland, amiable face. A yawn split it open.

'Here it is.' She fished about inside the blue plastic bag that they had had with them in the aeroplane and brought out a bottle of tablets. 'I put them in there in case you started a headache on the journey.'

Breathing hard, Leo pushed the gun down among

the socks and closed the lid of the suitcase on them. He muttered, 'Thanks.'

'Wait a minute,' she said. 'I'll get you a glass of water.'

As soon as she was in the bathroom, running the water until it came fairly cold, he opened the case again, whipped the gun out of it, rolled it in a pullover that he could not possibly need in this heat and thrust them to the back of the top shelf of the wardrobe cupboard. Melanie was not a tall woman. She would not think of reaching up to put anything else there.

She came back with a glass of water.

'I suppose it's all right to drink the water here,' she said. 'If the British didn't leave much else behind them when they went, they probably left a good water supply. Shall I ring for breakfast now, or d'you want to give the pills time to work first?'

'Just as you like. Now, if you want to.'

Leo swallowed two tablets, made his way back to his bed, lay down and buried his face in the pillow.

He heard Melanie pick up the telephone and ask for two breakfasts to be sent to their room. Then she began to wander about, beginning to do some unpacking. Leo wondered what she would have done if she had come on the gun. Putting it in the suitcase had of course been a risk, but he had thought that the chance of the cases being opened between London and Nicosia was small. He had known that ever since all that hi-jacking trouble the hand-baggage of passengers going to the Near East was searched before they left Heathrow, and in fact Melanie had had to open her handbag and the blue plastic bag, and they had had to walk through an electro-magnetic beam between two posts, which somehow or other would have revealed it if they had been carrying any object made of metal. A man just in front of Leo had been stopped and questioned because he had had what had turned out to be a big bunch of keys in his pocket. But neither of the suitcases had had to be opened on the journey. That they might be examined in some way like the hand luggage was a risk Leo had decided to take. And everything had gone just as he had hoped. When he and Melanie had arrived in Nicosia there had been no one on earth who knew that he possessed a gun. The first part of his plan had been achieved completely successfully.

But then he had left the gun in the open case all night ...

In spite of the heat, he shivered.

He had found the gun one day, and the ammunition too, in the dusty loft of a tall, decrepit house in the old part of the town where he and Melanie had their antique shop. They had just bought up the contents of the house for the sake of the few good pieces in it, when the widow who had lived there for thirty years had died. They often made that kind of deal with executors after a death, disposing of the rubbish in the house in one of the cheaper salerooms, and they always went very carefully through what they found in lofts. For astonishing things could sometimes be found there. More than once they had discovered quite valuable things, jewellery, old silver, old books, the existence of which their owners seemed to have forgotten. Once they had found a bottle of potassium cyanide, enough to kill off a whole family, with a few dead moths in it. They had found very compromising letters and once an unexplained skull. At one time Melanie had searched as diligently through these things as Leo. But lately she had grown reluctant to climb ladders, saying it made her head swim, and it had come about that Leo had been alone when he had found the gun, found it and slipped it swiftly, furtively, hardly knowing why he was doing it, back into its box and put it on one side, among the other things up there that had seemed to be worth keeping. Later he had put the box on a shelf in the storeroom behind the shop, a shelf which was too high for Melanie to reach without climbing one of those step-ladders that she did not like. And there it had stayed for six months. . . .

'Beautiful morning this morning,' the waiter who brought them their breakfast told them happily. He was small and brown-skinned, with a wide smile and big, dark, sparkling eyes. 'Fine sunshine. Beautiful.'

'Isn't it always beautiful here?' Melanie asked. 'The advertisements say so.'

'Ah no, not always,' the waiter said, looking as if it saddened him inexpressibly to damage such a charming illusion. 'Very changeable. Last week we had storm. Great wind, rain, terrible. But no storm today. Sunshine, everything beautiful.'

As he went out Melanie said, 'They're very friendly, aren't they? They don't seem to have anything against us now, whatever they had in the past.'

'Only against each other,' Leo answered. 'Greeks and Turks, water and oil. Each lot would like to finish the others off. I can't think why the rest of us don't let them get on with it. What's the coffee like?' Strong coffee sometimes helped with his headaches.

'Pretty watery,' Melanie said when she had poured some out and sipped it. 'That waiter was a Greek, wouldn't you say? I thought he had a Greek sort of look about him.'

'Couldn't tell the difference myself.' Leo sat up, reaching for the cup that she held out to him. 'Oh God, this stuff is muck!'

'And the toast's soggy,' Melanie said, swinging her

bare feet as she sat on the edge of her bed. 'But why worry? It's wonderful to be here, isn't it? And if you don't feel like driving to Kyrenia to see Uncle Ben this morning, we can go in the afternoon. I was looking in the guide-book last night and it's only about fifteen or sixteen miles from Nicosia. Actually, it might be better to go in the afternoon, because then it won't look as if we expect to be given lunch. D'you know, I'm really looking forward to seeing the old boy again. I miss him.'

The telephone rang.

Melanie picked it up, listened, replied, put it down again and said, 'It's someone from the travel agency. They'll deliver the car to us here at ten-thirty.'

'I'm not going anywhere till this head clears,' Leo said.

'I'll drive,' Melanie said. 'You needn't worry. They drive on the left here, don't they, like reasonable people?'

'Just leave me in peace for a bit, can't you?' Leo said. 'I'll be all right presently.'

In fact, it was mid-afternoon when the two of them got into the hired car and set out to find the road north-wards to Kyrenia, where Melanie's Uncle Ben had lived for the last year. They began by losing their way and found themselves in the old Turkish city at the heart of Nicosia, a place of intricately interwoven one-way streets, old houses that overhung the pavements, blazing horns and throngs of pedestrians who strolled across the streets, right in front of the car, without considering for a moment, so it seemed, that this might put their lives in danger. The car was appallingly hot from having stood in the sunshine for several hours. The sky was a glittering arch of unbroken blue.

Leo drove. He was an aggressive, bad-tempered

driver. By the time that he had extricated the car from the old city and found the wide road that curved around it outside the walls, he was abusing all other drivers, all pedestrians and Melanie, for having failed to read the map correctly.

'Never mind,' she said in her calm way, 'we aren't in any hurry. Now we've got to find that turning on the right. It ought to be coming quite soon, if we haven't passed it already.'

'Well, for God's sake, keep your eyes peeled!'

A minute or two later they came to a big roundabout and saw the road to Kyrenia branching off it. Leo swung into it and speeded up. But almost immediately the road narrowed and then was obstructed by a barricade of oil drums. Leo had to bring the car almost to a standstill before a dark-haired, dark-skinned man in uniform waved them on through a gap in the barricade.

'What was that about, d'you suppose?' Melanie asked as they speeded up again afterwards. 'It was almost like a frontier, wasn't it? D'you think that's what it was? I mean, have we just gone from Greek into Turkish territory, or the other way round? What do you think he was, that policeman, Greek or Turkish?'

'I can't tell the difference, I told you, and I couldn't care less, so long as they don't bother us,' Leo answered.

'Well, I can tell the difference,' Melanie said after a moment. 'This is Turkish where we are. The names over the shops are all written in ordinary letters. But the Greeks use the Greek alphabet, don't they?'

They drove on towards the open country.

It was flat at first, a lot of it boggy-looking waste land, with fields of barley here and there and a few blue patches of flax. Most of it had a rather desolate air. The fields were empty, and except for an occasional cyclist, there was not much traffic. But all of a sudden, coming from the direction of Kyrenia, they saw two army jeeps. Both had their headlights on, looking like sickly, jaundiced eyes in the brilliance of the afternoon sunshine. The soldiers in the jeeps wore light blue berets, and all of them were blonde, almost startlingly so in this island of dark people. On each jeep was a plate that read, 'United Nations.' Then behind them, one after the other, nose to tail in an astonishing stream, came cars, ordinary cars, not army vehicles of any kind, but Austins, Morrises, Vauxhalls, Volkswagens, large and small, and all filled with ordinary-looking people in everyday clothes, not in uniform.

'Goodness,' Melanie said, 'I shouldn't have thought there were so many cars in Cyprus. I suppose they've got held up by those jeeps going so slowly for some reason.'

'I'd say it looks like a convoy,' Leo replied.

Another jeep appeared, also filled with blonde men in blue berets, and after it the road was suddenly empty again.

'But what would people like that be doing in a convoy?' Melanie asked. 'Most of them look just as if they're going home from a day by the sea. Oh, here come some more. . . .'

Another pair of jeeps with headlights on was coming towards them. But this time the jeeps were followed only by lorries, the stream ending, as before, with a third jeep.

'Quaint local custom, that's all,' Leo said.

He glanced at his watch. It was about twenty minutes since they had left the hotel. But if they had not got lost first in the old town, they would not have taken as long. It might be important to remember that. He had better notice precisely how long the drive took between Nicosia and Kyrenia.

For the last few miles the road twisted snakily downwards between bare rocky hills. They passed a military post of some sort, manned by armed, dark men in uniform. Then ahead was the sea.

They drove slowly into the little town, finding themselves on a road curving round the harbour, with tables under bright umbrellas on the esplanade between the road and the water. Ahead of them was the high, blank wall of the old Crusader castle. As they crept along a telephone booth caught Leo's eye. Bright red and exactly the same as any telephone booth in London. Last, irrelevant remnant of an empire.

'We'll have to ask the way,' Melanie said. 'I've a feeling we've got lost again.'

Leo pulled up, called out to a passer-by and asked for directions.

It turned out that what Leo and Melanie had been told about everyone in Cyprus speaking English was largely a legend. The man whom Leo addressed could manage about half a dozen words. But he made up for it with a lot of pointing and arm-waving. Leo turned the car, as this seemed to be indicated, then soon asked the way again. It was another ten minutes before he found the way to the villa on the edge of the town, where Uncle Ben lived.

But if you knew the way, Leo thought, half an hour from door to door would be enough. Half an hour was what he must allow for.

They found Uncle Ben lying in a cane chair on the terrace overlooking his garden. He looked tanned and healthy and he got to his feet quite nimbly when they appeared. Yet he did not look particularly glad to see them. As usual, he looked ready to find fault, to charge them with deliberately upsetting him.

'I thought you were coming this morning,' he said. 'Mrs Nicolaou got together all the doings for lunch. She's the woman who looks after me. But I suppose you wanted a slap-up meal in your hotel.'

Melanie kissed him.

'Leo had one of his headaches,' she said. 'He isn't used to the heat yet. You ought to have a telephone, then we could have let you know.'

'Who'd use it, if I had one?' Uncle Ben said in his self-pitying whine. 'Useless expense.'

'Haven't you made any friends here, then?' she asked.

'I'm too old to make new friends,' he replied. 'I can't be bothered with strangers.'

'You must be lonely.'

'Oh, I'm all right. The climate helps my arthritis, there's no question of that. I don't complain.' His tone complained bitterly.

'You've a lovely place here,' Leo said. 'I envy you, Uncle Ben.'

It was not true. The villa was very small, a mere suburban bungalow, standing cheek by jowl with its identical neighbours. Its cream-coloured walls were blotchy. In its garden the canna lilies, geraniums and marigolds sprouted among dense, vigorous weeds.

Yet Uncle Ben had money and could easily have had the place spruced up if he had not been too mean. He had had thirty thousand pounds left to him by his sister Gertrude. For Melanie there had been only some hideous silver and one thousand pounds, but for Ben, who had never bothered about Gertrude, or anyone else, for that matter, there had been a small fortune. And instead of repaying Melanie and Leo for having looked after him ever since the death of his wife, three years before, he had merely said that at least he could now afford to take himself off their hands and stop being a burden to them, and that he had heard the climate of Cyprus was recommended for arthritis.

Six months later Leo had found the gun in the attic. . . .

'But how do you manage?' Melanie asked. 'I mean about the cooking and cleaning and so on? This Mrs Nicholas, does she live in?'

'Nicolaou,' Uncle Ben corrected her. 'She comes in the morning, keeps the place like a new pin, gets my lunch and washes up and leaves my supper ready. She's a widow, no children, glad to have the occupation, I expect. She's very obliging, very good-natured, as so many of them are here, you know. Wonderfully warm-hearted people. She's fine-looking too.'

He smirked a little as he said it and Leo noticed suddenly that Melanie was trying to catch his eye and was raising her eyebrows.

On the way back to Nicosia she said, 'You don't think there's any risk he's fallen for that woman, do you?'

'Good Lord, it never occurred to me,' Leo said. 'Good luck to him if he has.'

'But the way he looked when he talked about her. . . . And living here, cut off from us all, and without any friends, he just might go and do something silly.'

'Well, perhaps it was a good idea of yours to come and visit him – remind him we're alive, so to speak.'

'I thought it was your idea,' Melanie said.

'Oh no, it was yours,' Leo said quickly. He wanted her to be sure that it had been. 'Now where shall we eat tonight? And what shall we do tomorrow? Go swimming?'

They had found out from Uncle Ben that there was a good beach, a long, unblemished strip of white sand, not far from Kyrenia.

'Or shall we go sight-seeing?' Leo asked. 'We could go to Famagusta, where Othello hung out, the guide-book says, or there's that Greek place, Salamis, with baths and a gymnasium, and all that sort of thing.'

'Let's see how we feel tomorrow,' Melanie answered.

Leo knew how he was going to feel tomorrow. He was going to have another headache. But there was no need to tell her so now.

He woke her in the morning by blundering around the room, looking for the codeine tablets. She got up quickly and fetched them from the bathroom cabinet, together with a glass of water. Leo went back to bed, burrowed his face into the pillow and shut his eyes.

'But look,' he mumbled, 'there's no need for you to stay around just because I'm stuck here. Why don't you get yourself a picnic lunch and take the car and go to that beach Uncle Ben told us about? Swim and enjoy yourself. Then perhaps you could drop in again on the old boy in the afternoon and see if you think he's really getting into the toils of that female he talked about.'

'Well, if you wouldn't mind being left. . . .'

'Of course not. No need to waste your time here just because my damned head's playing up.'

'Then if you're really sure. . . .'

He said that he was sure and soon after breakfast Melanie left, with her swimming things and a packed lunch provided by the hotel.

As soon as she had gone, Leo got up and dressed. He went down in the lift and out into the street. He was wearing his sunglasses and a straw hat. But the first thing he did was to buy another pair of sunglasses, bigger than the ones that he had on, more in the fashion of the moment, more face-concealing. Then he bought a little hat of stitched red cotton with a brim that could be turned down all round. With these purchases he returned to his room, put the packages on the top shelf of the cupboard, where the gun was hidden, then lay down on the bed again, gazed up at the ceiling and began to work out the details of his plan. For of course he had not been able to do that until he got here.

Keep it simple, he thought. At all costs, keep it simple. And the main things to remember are that that Cypriot woman stays in the house until she's washed up the lunch things, which probably means two o'clock, and that the drive between Kyrenia and Nicosia takes about half an hour. And of course that no one on earth knows that you've got a gun. Always remember that.

When Melanie returned to the hotel in the late afternoon, she was looking sombre. She asked how Leo's headache was, but when he told her that it had quite gone by lunch-time and that he had gone prowling around the Cathedral of Saint Sophia she did not look as if she were listening. She hung up her damp swimsuit in the bathroom, and slowly, frowningly, changed her dress for the evening. The sun had already scorched her fair skin, turning it brick red where it had not been covered by the swimsuit. She hardly spoke until she was seated at the dressing-table, trying to brush the sand and salt out of her hair.

Abruptly then she said, 'You know, I really believe that silly old thing has fallen for that woman.'

Leo laughed.

She slapped her hand smartly with the hairbrush, as if she would have liked to slap Leo.

'I wish you wouldn't take it as a joke,' she said. 'I'm

horribly afraid it's serious.'

'Well, it's his life, isn't it?'

'Oh, it isn't that I grudge him some happiness, poor old boy,' she said. 'He led a dog's life with Aunt Tina, and then the arthritis hitting him when he was naturally so active was terrible bad luck. He's always had terrible bad luck, hasn't he, except for getting Aunt Gertrude's money? And now I don't want to see some scheming, half-educated sort of woman get that out of him. But the way he talked ... Mrs Nicolaou this and Mrs Nicolaou that. ... And then how lonely he was, and how life as it was wasn't worth living. I suggested he should come back to us, if that was how he felt, but he wouldn't hear of it. Honestly, I'm worried.'

'Depressed, was he?' Leo said.

'Well, sort of moody, up one moment, down the next.'

'He was always a bit like that, as far as I remember.'

'Yes, but I think it's worse. He hasn't made friends among the other English residents, there's just this woman.'

'Well, we'll have to see what we can do to take his mind off her for the next week or two,' Leo said, 'only we'd better not overdo it, or he'll think we're after his money ourselves.'

Melanie sighed. 'I wouldn't mind some of it, that's the honest truth. But mainly I just don't want him to make a fool of himself. And for all I know, this Mrs Nicolaou is as nice as he says. But still. ... Oh dear, no, I'm being a hypocrite, aren't I? Of course it's the money I'm worried about. I've been so sure he'd no one to leave it to but us. Wouldn't it be *awful* if he just gave it away to a stranger?'

Leo had an extraordinary impulse at that moment to put his arms round her, caress her, cheer her, tell her that she had nothing to worry about, and tell her his plan. His beautifully simple, completed plan. He had always been deeply attached to Melanie and during all their years together had had very few secrets from her. The gun had been almost the first. So now, for him, it would have been a wonderful relief from tension to tell her what he had in his mind and to feel, since they both wanted the same thing, that they could work together.

But of course it would not do. It would not be fair on Melanie. Besides, she was a very clumsy liar, so it was important that when the time came, she should have to tell only what she believed was the truth. Instead of reaching for her, Leo thrust one hand out before him and opened and closed the fingers, as if he were grasping at something. In a detached sort of way, it impressed him that his hand was completely steady.

Next day they drove to Paphos on the south coast and looked at the mosaic flooring of the House of Dionysos, and photographed one another among the Tombs of the Kings. On the day after that they drove up into the Troodos mountains, the wild range where the terrorists had sheltered during the time of the troubles. Suddenly the car was enveloped in a shower of sleet. Leo and Melanie found themselves shivering in their light summer clothing. The next day they did nothing in particular, except idle round the shops, where Melanie wanted to buy some of the lace of the island, look for a place for lunch that promised to be interesting and then spend a drowsy afternoon sleeping off the excellent but immense meal that they had unwarily let themselves in for. It was on the day after that that Leo suggested that they might call in again on Uncle Ben.

They did not lose their way this time, but stuck to the road outside the walls of the old city, found the roundabout and the turning off it to Kyrenia, passed through the barricade of oil drums, drove on along the road through the Turkish village beyond, then on across the desolate plain, passing the military post where the armed men in charge of it impassively watched them go by, then dipping down between the jagged hills towards the sea. As the car entered the outskirts of Kyrenia Leo looked at his watch. Yes, half an hour, as near as made no difference.

They did not go straight to Uncle Ben's house but went first to the beach to which Melanie had gone before and spent what was left of the morning swimming and lying in the sun. They ate their lunch of sand-wiches and fruit in the shade of some bamboos and drank the bottle of wine that they had bought before setting out. An unusual sense of peace and well-being filled Leo. His body felt relaxed, his mind calm and clear. His nerves were untroubled. He felt a kind of omniscience too, the certitude that nothing could go wrong with his plan. Pulling Melanie towards him, he kissed her with a sudden warmth that seemed to leave her a little surprised at him.

They found Uncle Ben in the cane chair on the terrace of his little house.

'So you've come again,' the old man said. 'I thought you'd forgotten me.'

'We don't want to be a bother,' Melanie said. 'We don't want to be a pest.'

'You don't want to be bothered, that's the truth of it,' Uncle Ben answered. 'You had more than enough of that in the old days. But now you're actually here in Cyprus for a couple of weeks, you might give me an occasional thought. I don't have many visitors. I just sit here day after day and wonder how I'm going to get through it.'

'Well, I said, didn't I,' Melanie said, 'you can always come back to us?'

'It's too late,' he answered. 'I'm too old for another upheaval. Besides, the climate *is* good for the arthritis. And I dare say I'll settle down sooner or later. I've started learning Greek. It helps to pass the time. I'm taking lessons in the evenings from a very good chap who lives up the road and I practice on Mrs Nicolaou. She laughs at me but she's very patient, very good-natured. A dear soul, a treasure. I don't know where I'd be without her.'

He's doing it on purpose, Leo thought. He wants us to worry about how far he means to go with her.

They left at about four o'clock. Melanie was pre-occupied. Leo had his own reasons for remaining silent. They soon caught up with a United Nations jeep, filled with blonde young men in pale blue berets. Leo tried to pass it, but was waved imperiously back, which irritated him and made him mutter, 'Who the hell do they think they are?' But passing the jeep would not have been much use, for ahead of it was a long string of lorries. Leo had to accept the fact that he must fall in behind the jeep and crawl slowly along all the way to Nicosia.

The next day Leo and Melanie went to Famagusta and roamed round the old Turkish town, photograph-ing mosques and churches and the lion of Venice on the gateway of the building called Othello's Tower. They wanted to climb the steps up the tower, but these were blocked all the way up by a solid mass of other tourists who had come off a ship in the harbour. Melanie sat down on a slab of stone in the courtyard before the tower and prepared to wait until the party had gone. She was hot, she said, and her feet were tired, so it was quite nice to sit down. But Leo was in an impatient mood today, restless and nervous because the time for action was coming close, and after a few minutes of listening to the astonishingly penetrating voice of the guide, explaining that Othello had not really been a black man at all, he insisted on moving on.

On the drive back to Nicosia, across the great flat plain that spread over the central part of the island, Leo said, 'I suppose we may as well go to Kyrenia again tomorrow, if the old boy really wants us. We could do what we did yesterday, swim, have lunch and drop in on him in the afternoon. Shall we do that?'

'If you like,' Melanie answered.

'He seemed so depressed yesterday,' Leo said. 'I was quite worried.'

'Oh, he was always given to being sorry for himself.' Melanie was looking to left and right. 'Have you noticed how few people you see working in the fields? Just a few old women. I suppose all the young men are in those frightful armies, just waiting for a chance to start shooting at one another.'

Leo did not want to change the subject yet. 'I thought he was a good deal more depressed than usual. More than he used to be, even if his arthritis is better.'

'I dare say,' Melanie agreed. 'All right, let's go and see him tomorrow. Funny, though, I thought he bored you terribly.'

'Somehow I can't help feeling sorry for him,' Leo said. 'And I expect we'll both be pretty boring ourselves when we're his age and have his arthritis of whatever else afflicts us then.'

'You used not to be so tolerant. If you had been, perhaps he wouldn't have felt he'd got to go away.'

Annoyed, Leo said, 'I don't think that had anything to do with it. He just didn't want to let us have any of his money. So serves him right if he's miserable.'

Melanie gave him a sidelong look. 'You're funny,' she said. 'I don't understand you.'

She had said the same thing frequently for the last twenty years. Leo had long ago given up trying to explain himself to her.

That night he could not sleep. Lying awake, staring tired-eyed at the darkness, he felt an enormous weariness at the mere thought of finally taking decisive action. How much easier, how much pleasanter it would be to forget that he had ever had a plan and just enjoy the rest of the holiday, like any ordinary person. The old man could not live so very much longer anyhow. Nature would take its course. The money then would come to Melanie. But suppose, just suppose, the old fool went and married that woman . . .

The hours passed slowly.

With the morning a shaft of sunlight crept across their beds, striped by the slats of the Venetian blind. It wakened Melanie, who opened her eyes, blinked them at the brightness, glanced at her watch, mumbled something about its still being too early to order breakfast and shut them again.

Leo gave a groan.

'What's the trouble?' she asked.

'My head,' he said. 'Oh God, my head!'

'Bad?'

'Absolute hell.'

'It's this heat,' she said. 'I'm afraid it doesn't suit you. Next year we'll have to stick to Torquay. Want the codeine?'

'If you wouldn't mind . . .'

She swung her feet down to the floor. Leo heard her padding about the room, heard her run water in the bathroom as she filled a glass, heard her come to his bedside. He raised his head, took the two tablets she held out to him, gulped some water, then buried his face in the pillow again. Melanie went back to bed and almost immediately dropped asleep. It was nearly nine o'clock before she woke once more and ordered breakfast.

When it came, brought by the small, dark, smiling waiter, Leo drank a cup of coffee but refused to eat anything. When Melanie suggested that going to Kyrenia and having a swim might help, he demanded that for God's sake she should leave him alone.

'But you go,' he said. 'Take the car. Take your lunch. Have a swim yourself. Go to see the old man. Just leave me alone.'

'But it's not so much fun, all by oneself,' she said.

'It won't be much fun for you either, hanging around here.'

'Well, if you're sure ...'

'Of course I'm sure. You can't help.'

She did not take much persuading.

It was half past ten when she took the car and drove off to Kyrenia. Leo did not hurry after she had gone, but presently got up, dressed, went out and strolled about the town for a little while, so that the maid could do the room, then returned to it, lay down again and spent a quiet morning reading. At half past twelve he went to the bar and had a drink. He did not linger over it, but he had a chat with the barman about the composition of a brandy sour, which seemed to be the favourite drink in the place, and thought that the man would remember that he had been there. At a quarter to one Leo went to the dining room and again made a point of chatting to the waiter. At a quarter past one he went to his room, took the red cotton hat and the big black sunglasses from the top shelf of the cupboard, put a pair of gloves in his pocket, made a bundle of his swimming trunks and a towel and put the gun in the middle of it. Then he went down in the lift, out to the street, turned to the right, turned again to the right, so that he was out of sight of the hotel, put on the red hat and the sunglasses and hailed a taxi.

He told the driver that he wanted to go to Kyrenia and they set off along the road outside the old town, came to the roundabout, took the turning to Kyrenia, passed through the gap in the oil-drum barricade and drove on along the road across the plain.

The driver, a stout, hunched figure of a man, had a sullen sort of talkativeness. He told Leo that he was a Turk and went on to tell him what a miserable thing it was to be a Turk in Cyprus, with the Greeks getting all the best jobs and just waiting for a chance to murder you. His complaints, in halting, mumbling English, went on for most of the drive. Leo did not listen. Now that the time had come, now that so soon there would be no turning back, he did not feel conscious fear, but only a chilly kind of rigidity. He paid off the taxi at the harbour in Kyrenia, sat down at a table there under a bright umbrella and ordered a beer, drank it quickly, then walked along the road to Uncle Ben's house. There was a bench near the house, which he had noticed on his first visit. Sitting down on it, he lit a cigarette. The time was a few minutes after two o'clock.

It was a quarter past two when Mrs Nicolaou left the house. She was a dark-skinned, dumpy woman in a tight, printed cotton dress. She had a fluffed out mass of black hair and walked with little mincing steps. She did not even glance at Leo. As soon as she was out of sight, he got up, slipped on his gloves, turned in at the gate of Uncle Ben's house, walked round the house to the terrace at the back, saw Uncle Ben lying there in his cane chair, half-asleep, held the gun to his temple and shot him.

Leo had forgotten about the noise. The sight of death did not frighten him, for he had seen enough of it to be hardened during the war. But as he heard the angry bark of the gun in his hand, he felt his first real fear. But the echo died and silence followed. Somewhere not far away a hen cackled loudly, but that was the only sign of disturbance. Leo tugged at one of the old man's limp hands, folded it round the gun, then dropped the gun on the ground beside his chair, with the hand dangling above it, as if the gun had just fallen from the fingers. Then he walked quietly away round the house, out into the street and strolled back to the harbour.

He had no difficulty in finding another taxi to take him back to Nicosia. It was as he got into it that he began to shake. Collapsing on the seat, closing his eyes, he trembled from head to foot. Tensing his muscles, he tried to fight it. But that only made it worse. Yet something must be done, or the driver might notice it. Deliberately Leo tried to relax, and to calm himself, started to go over in his head everything that he had done, to tell himself how well it had gone.

First, if anyone had seen him sitting on the bench or entering the house, it would be the red hat and the outsize sunglasses that he would remember. There was no risk that he would be recognised.

Second, no one could ever trace that gun to him. No one in the world knew that he had ever possessed it. It had probably lain in that loft since at least the war, its very existence forgotten. So how could anything ever be proved against him?

Third, luckily for Leo, Uncle Ben had made a parade of his loneliness and depression. Certainly not only to Leo and Melanie, but to Mrs Nicolaou too, and his other acquaintances. What more likely, then, that one day he would kill himself? How had he got hold of the gun? Well, hadn't there been a time when guns had been common in Cyprus? Weren't they still, if it came to that? You had only to look about you.

Fourth, by the time that Melanie had had her lunch after her swim, slept for a little in the shade of the bamboos, driven to the house, arriving, say, at about three o'clock, found the body and rushed out in terror to the nearest of those red telephone booths to call Leo, he would be safely back in his room in the hotel, ready to answer the call. The red hat and the sunglasses would have been disposed of in some litter-bin, or just dropped in the gutter, as soon as he had paid off the taxi. He would be terribly shocked and upset at what Melanie told him, would tell her to get hold of the first policeman she could find, and that he himself would come to her as quickly as he was able. And he would make quite sure that the people in the hotel knew that he had received that call. . . .

Boldness. Simplicity. What could go wrong?

The trembling gradually ceased. He opened his eyes to look at his watch. It was twenty-five minutes to three. That left plenty of time.

But something suddenly bewildered him. The taxi should have been climbing the steep, twisting road through the hills. Instead it was speeding along a flat, straight road with the sea on the right of it, calm, glittering, serene. There were mountains on the left, but nowhere near the road.

Leo shot forward to the edge of the seat and grabbed the driver's shoulder.

'Here, where are we? Where are you taking me?' he shouted.

'To Nicosia,' the man answered. 'You want to go to Nicosia, no?'

'But this isn't the way!'

'It is the way.'

'It isn't. I've never come this way. You're playing some trick on me.'

'No trick. This is the only way I can take you. I am a Greek. On the other road there is a Turkish village. I am not allowed to drive through it.'

'What do you mean, you're not allowed?'

'What I say. Haven't you seen the sentries and the oil drums? The Turks say, if we let you come into our villages, you will kill us. It is not true, but it is what they say. A Greek cannot go to Nicosia by the other road unless he goes in a United Nations convoy. They go twice a day, nine in the morning and four in the afternoon, with jeeps before and behind. But this is a nice drive. No need to worry.'

At that moment Leo saw a road-sign ahead of them. It said, 'Nicosia, 44.' Forty-four miles! *Forty-four ...!* It might easily take an hour. And Melanie would find Uncle Ben, would telephone the hotel, would be told there was no answer ...

And he had thought that it did not matter if you could not tell the difference between a Greek and a Turk!

'Oh, God, God!' Leo cried pounding his knees with his fists, panic making his voice almost a scream. 'This can't happen! You can't do this to me!'

'No need to worry,' the driver repeated placidly. 'It costs you no more than going the short way.'

THE BORE

by Joan Fleming

The girl, who had been round my neck all evening, finally raised her lovely eyes to mine and asked the inevitable question: 'Are you married?' she said. I stared back at her, stared because my eyes were nearly out of focus, she kept receding into the distance.

'I was,' I croaked.

'How do you mean ... was?'

How did I mean *was*? It was the kind of idiotic question Sabina would have asked! *How did I mean was?* 'She's dead,' I said, just like that.

'Oh, I'm sorry,' the girl said, meaning she was glad.

There were only half a dozen of us at the party and as dinner had just been announced there was an expectant silence in the few seconds duration in which my voice rang out loud and clear: 'I killed her,' I explained, and then I added: 'Because she was so damned dull.'

Well, American sense of humour is in a different key from ours, as we all know; they're all a bit chippy and don't quite know how to take us but this was a piece of straight fun and caused the first good laugh I made that trip.

'Come on in to dinner,' the host said, when the laugh was over, hand on my shoulder. I took a furtive look at myself as we passed through the tiny hall on the wall of which was a large landscape looking glass. I didn't look in the least drunk, my hair was smooth, my face stern even and presently I was being served avocado mousse by a soft-footed Negro man-servant and

The Girl, sitting next to me, was asking me if we had avocados in England. I was thinking up something intensely witty about the fruit having just reached our off-shore isle when the other male guest led the attention away from me by talking about their last summer holiday in a Greek Island which, by one of those absolutely evil coincidences, happened to be Kolynos.

Or perhaps it wasn't quite such a coincidence; the islands are invaded in turn, and 'developed' more and more as people seek the smaller unspoilt ones, claiming one or other as their own particular 'find'. If you press them to tell you the name they won't but sooner or later, if you ask them if they are going to their favourite island again, they tell you sadly: 'Well, it's been *found*, I'm afraid.'

After the mousse there was grilled fillets of sole and the other male guest was still going on about Kolynos and the gorgeous fish they had had at the new little hotel that had recently been opened.

Then everyone started talking about their visits to the Greek Islands, not to be outdone and since I'd visited them long before it became smart to have been there, I joined in, it was easier to do so than to remain silent. The drinks had made me, among other things, boastful and I heard myself claim that I had known Kolynos when no visitors had ever been there, staying in one of the cottages almost on the shore. I was too far gone in drink at the time to notice that the other male guest was having a particularly careful look at me, but I registered and remember it now.

As I can't remember ever mentioning the damned place in all the years since we were there, I can only explain my indiscretion by what I had said before the meal. The mind seems to work like that, the one thing you know you mustn't mention is suddenly the one thing you find yourself talking about. And if you're off your guard, well, anything can happen.

And did.

Excellent though the meal was I found difficulty in swallowing it. Ten years, ten successful, busy years and I had to come out with it, just like that! And I hadn't even thought of it for years! Talk about alcohol stirring up the id!

But I was desperately worried, if I could come out entirely unexpectedly with a thing like that, when would I do it again? I'm forty, middle-aged, I have to admit; a lonely (sic) widower or, more truthfully, a widower who lives alone, in great ease and comfort. Too much ease, probably, a fit subject for a coronary thrombosis. Or a stroke. Or perhaps I was suddenly to go off my rocker.

It was like this, the agency had opened a new office in Ohio and I had flown over to see the thing properly on its feet and stopped off, as they call it, in New York on the way back. A client of ours, with a penthouse flat in Park Avenue, had given this small party for me, inviting me at six-thirty and filling me up with icy cold highballs for a couple of hours before any food appeared.

Instead of being elated by the drinks I became more and more morose and the unmarried girl they had asked for my benefit was unspeakably dull and reminded me intensely of Sabina ... but Hell's bells!

For the rest of the meal I don't think I registered anything, I was so immersed in my thoughts: I was twenty-nine, an ambitious chap, going places; it is possible that the girls in the agency, secretaries and typists, are even more attractive now, in their mediaeval-page tabards with all their thighs showing, than they were then; it all goes over my head now, I don't even see them. I can't be bothered.

Sabina had been there several weeks before I saw her, taking shorthand notes in an office into which I rarely went.

I hadn't by any means had a surfeit of girls in my life and that was probably half the trouble, once I fell in love I really had it badly. I was obsessed by her. I asked her then and there if she'd come out for a drink with me in half-an-hour's time and the chap I'd called in to see said: 'Watch it, Sabina, he's the Wolf of the Media department!' giving me a wink. And she ignored him and said: 'Well, if you're sure ...'

Of course I was sure.

So an hour later we were sitting in the Westway bar and she was telling me about her hair; when she was at school it was short and then when she left school she grew it, and it grew and grew, and finally she could sit on it.

'Sit on it!' I gaped.

Yes, she could sit on it.

'Well, I never,' I must have said.

But then the plot thickened and finally, she had this marvellous hair cut off ...

'Then everyone could sit on it,' I must have said but she brushed that aside and told me she had it made into a switch or a tail or whatever they are called, and all this and all that.

A week later I asked her to marry me.

She didn't ask for time to think about it, she said yes, then and there.

We married. She was mine, my own precious, marvellous, unspeakably glorious, own, own alabaster beaker, as it were.

'You know,' she mused, 'I don't know how it is, but I knew you were the right person, just as soon as I saw you, I thought, that's him . . .'

   'He!'

   'What?'

   'Oh nothing!'

'You're such a funny darling,' she smiled. 'Oh, look at that lovely sunset, maybe I didn't need to bring my drizzle boots after all, they do take up such a lot of room in my new case.'

Walking hand-in-hand through Pompeii she told me all about her kid brother and the trouble they had with his aneuresis and how he had been completely cured by a bell which her father had fixed up from wall to wall which . . .

In Athens she was still glorious, but glorious, and as we climbed up to the Acropolis she leaped from rock to rock like a young hart telling me all the time about how she and another girl had had this crush on . . .

But we were on our way: a boat took us through the Archipelago, chugging along as it threaded its way in and out and round the enchanting islands, big and small and some of them mere rocks and I heard all about how five of them went on a camping tour in Snowdonia and it rained all the time so . . .

Kolynos had a row of white cottages with faded pale green doors and shutters and we went to one of them and asked for accommodation; the woman said she took in guests and there was a cafe on the shore. We stayed.

We lay side by side on the rocks and I watched her go a marvellous almond brown while she wondered how her pony was getting on and whether he was missing her . . .

Then one day I yawned, I never yawn, or hardly ever; when you're switched on, you don't yawn. But I couldn't stop, once I had started. I yawned and yawned. The spell was broken. Worse, I wandered away by myself and lay on rocks alone. She didn't seem to mind.

And then, and then, oh! it was enough to make the gods weep: I didn't even look forward to bedtime. And next I began to worry terribly about myself.

We drank too much wine; well, she did. She liked the resin they will put in their wine and she liked the ouzo or whatever they call it and on our last day, she overdid it, after lunch she was glassy-eyed and as I sat brooding darkly over my coffee in the beach cafe she jumped up and said she was going for a swim.

'Not here,' I begged her. 'Let's go to our own bit of beach.'

So we went. I said: 'Better not, after that meal,' but she went in. It was a tiny beach almost enclosed by rocks, you could dive into deep water, then swim out of the opening between the rocks into the wind and the waves. Sometimes we stayed in our private piscina and sometimes we swam out into the Aegean, this time she went alone but I followed after a few minutes.

As you might have expected she was yards away, further than she had ever gone. There was a chap with a tiny boat, fishing not so far off, he would have seen she was in trouble even more clearly than I, but I think he was asleep, bent over his line, back to me.

I'm a swimmer but not as good as all that, I'm not a life-saver, wouldn't know how to do it if I tried. I knew I couldn't save the poor kid so after yelling at the fisherman who seemed stone deaf, I simply turned and swam back to our piscina and that was that.

I lay there for a very long time, staring up at the brilliant sky through my dark glasses. Then I leaped to my feet, made the awful discovery that my wife was not beside me, rushed for help, organised a terrific search with everybody on the island willingly bringing out their boats and joining in.

Corpus delicti they call it in law, meaning the body is absent or something of the kind. The islanders couldn't possibly have been kinder or more sympathetic. I stayed on a week; there were various formalities to be undergone and when there was no point in staying any longer, I was taken off in a boat sent from the mainland, paid for by the authorities and it looked as though the entire inhabitants of the island came down on to the shore to see me off.

I promised to return of course and at the time I meant it.

And that is what I was recalling until somehow or other the dinner came to an end; I am afraid I was a disappointing guest, they were talking shop by the end of it and I was left out of the conversation altogether.

Finally, when we were back in the living room I apologised, saying I had had an extremely busy day, which I had, and that the highballs weren't exactly what I was used to. Would they forgive me if I were to leave?

It broke up the party; the girl who was like Sabina was depressed, knowing she had failed to make any sort of hit with me, the host offered to take her home, I was left to walk back to my hotel and as it was round the corner, the other male guest offered to walk with me as I was not quite sure of the way.

He obviously wanted to do so and the reason was revealed as soon as we were out of earshot.

'You didn't kill her, you know,' he said.

I wasn't with him at all, my evening was over, I hoped, I was already in mind, half asleep. I was not prepared for a discussion on a subject which had been under the carpet for a very long time.

'What?' I said irritably.

'I said: you didn't kill her,' he shouted above the traffic noise.

'It comes to the same thing, drowning sounds better than killing, that's all.'

He took a grip of my arm as we crossed the road and arriving safely on the opposite pavement he kept hold of me: 'She's alive, I've met her, no one could help meeting her if they stopped off at Kolynos. Oh boy! Oh boy! She's be-autiful!'

Rooted to the pavement, traffic crawling past, he told me the lot.

That fisherman ... at the time I shouted he was unhooking a pretty big fish from his line so I could hardly expect him to attend to my cries for help. When he'd finished he looked up to see my wife obviously drowning and myself swimming hard in the opposite direction. He rowed to her and dragged her out of the sea when she was just about finished. He laid her on the bottom of the boat and, rough Greek peasant though he was, he gave her the Scout treatment, forcing her to be sick and (imagination this probably) giving her the Kiss of Life. However ... he's short and dark and hairy, a Mediterranean man, my companion called him.

'Irresistible to women,' he grinned with such a wry twist of his mouth I would have wanted to hear more if my own news had not been so fantastic.

The fisherman lived round the other side of the island, which wasn't far, with, of course, his widowed mother. 'He took his princess home' ... my chum went on, enjoying himself immensely, 'and they lived happily ever after. The widowed mother was with him utterly about keeping their mouths shut; what wife would want to return to a, well yes, murdering husband? She never communicated with her parents, she settled down to being the perfect "wife".

'She has five children and they have started up a small hotel, built by the fisherman with the help of friends; it's small but always full, known all over the Archipelago, "the little pub on Kolynos with the English hostess".'

But now I wanted to be alone to think it all over. I couldn't possibly say her 'death' had hung over me like a dark shadow all these years, it hadn't. But . . .

The chap with me was immensely amused by the situation. 'By law,' he chuckled as we walked towards my hotel, 'by law you could go over there and claim her; the Greeks are fussy about that kind of thing, a man's wife is a man's wife and that's that! How about it?'

'Did she actually tell you . . .?'

'She actually told me she'd had an English husband who left her to drown when they were on their honeymoon. She tells all her favourites but of course, nobody believes her. And another thing, if you start asking questions, such as, who was he? she shuts up; so you're safe there, if that's what you're worried about.'

'What does she look like, after all those kids?'

'Very fat, but that's the thing to be in Greece; I tell you, she's a raving beauty. She's got this marvellous long hair, worn down her back like a school-girl . . .'

'Could she sit on it?'

He gave me a curious neon-lit look; we had reached my hotel.

He said : 'I asked her what you were like.'

'You did?'

'She said it was a good thing in the end, the way things happened. You were good-looking, she said, but you were a bore. She said you would have killed her with boredom, if you hadn't found a better way. . . .'

THE HIRELINGS

by William Haggard

John Malcolmson looked through his telescope sight.
It was going to be a difficult shot. He hadn't been told
the name of the man whom his business it was now to
kill but he hadn't a doubt he could do it competently.
He was hidden in a pile of rubble on the roof of the
building they hadn't yet finished and all John could see
was his weapon's muzzle. That didn't disturb him, he
shot like an angel, which indeed was the reason they'd
thrown him the job. The other would probably move to
fire, perhaps pulling away a brick or two, and even if
he didn't do that John was confident he'd be a very
dead duck before his finger took the second pressure.
An aperture which showed a muzzle was also one
which a bullet could enter and John had unusual ammunition. He didn't have to hit the man's body, only
part of the stones and debris which covered it. The
fragmentation would do the rest and the result, though
effective, would not be elegant. In a way the thought
offended him, not the killing, which he had done
before, but the mess and the very untidy death. He
was a first class shot who took pride in his skill, but
John Malcolmson preferred to kill cleanly.

His radio came to life beside him and his scout in
the crowd began to talk.

'Control to Polly.'

'Polly receiving you.'

John Malcolmson thought the jargon stupid. His
scout was not a policeman in uniform, and openly to
use his transmitter he'd have slipped into a shop or

lavatory. So why not just say: 'John, it's Michael here.'
But he didn't; he played it like something on telly.

'Procession delayed.'

'How long?'

'Twelve minutes.'

'I suppose His Nibs was drunk again.'

The Control didn't answer, he was secretly scan-
dalised. It wasn't that he admired His Nibs whom he
knew, as most of the country knew, was a coarse and
irredeemable soak, but he was twenty-something in
line to the throne and once had been rather closer than
that. It was unseemly that a man like Malcolmson
should speak with what had sounded like levity. The
Control asked sourly:

'Are you all right?'

'Of course I am.'

'Object of exercise still in position?'

'If he isn't he's left his rifle behind him.'

'Then Control to Polly. Good luck and out.'

Malcolmson lay still on his mattress, waiting. He
had everything he could conceivably need, a superla-
tive rifle with marksman's telescope, a tripod and the
special rounds, sandwiches and a thermos of coffee. He
wouldn't have gone with the people he worked for if
he hadn't considered them coldly efficient. Like others
in this peculiar world he was a part-time man, not a
salaried hack. He had discovered that very early on –
the 007s were largely imaginary. There were the desk
men but only a regular handful, the half dozen on top
who made the decisions, then the experts they hired to
do the work – safebreakers, forgers, the odd man who
would kill. John would kill when he thought it was
decent to do so, but he wasn't the all-purpose assassin.
His weapon was the one he loved, the one he was out-
standingly good with. No knives, no karate, no horrible

hand guns. It was skill with a rifle which earned him his extras but it wasn't the money which paid the rent. For that he was happy to work in a bank. He was a realist, not a committed romantic.

Sir James, he remembered, had made it sound reasonable, or as reasonable as that world allowed. He had called the Duke of Worcester His Nibs, and he had done so perfectly naturally, without hint he was talking down to a hireling. Everyone else called the duke His Nibs and everyone else was fed up to the teeth with him. His death would relieve the public purse of a subvention which the Exchequer resented, but the fact remained he was highly connected, and connected with a capital C. His death would be a welcome economy but publicly it might be an embarrassment.

Especially if that death were murder and murder by people Sir James needn't mention.

Then why not watch the ports and nab him, the man who was going to do the killing?

Ah, it wasn't as easy as that, alas. The Special Branch was discreet and efficient, and most prominent men of That Organisation would be nailed within hours of their crossing St George's. But this couldn't be a prominent man who wouldn't possess the special skill. They could hide behind chimneys and shoot down soldiers, preferably with a screen of children, or put bombs in shops to murder housewives, but a single shot at a moving car, through a crowd or more likely from somewhere above it, was work for a top class marksman. Like Malcolmson.

No doubt that was right but why not avoid it all? The route of His Nibs' procession was known, and crowds could be watched and rooftops patrolled.

Sir James had acquiesced politely. That was per-

fectly true and he didn't deny it: in any normal circumstances the police would have done exactly that,
and he himself and Malcolmson too would not have
been discussing the matter. But the circumstances were
far from normal. Naturally he had information or they
wouldn't be sitting here drinking sherry, and the information was acutely embarrassing. For the killer would
not be an Englishman nor even a man from You Know
Where but a national of a major Power by whose protection, inexpert but still undeniable, the countries of
western Europe survived. Arrest such a man on mere
suspicion (his weapon would come in later and separ-
ately) and at once there'd be an appalling rumpus, not
a matter of two officials co-operating but one for the
over-zealous diplomats. And when lawyers and diplomats rattled their fetters the sensible citizen ran for
cover. This murder would be a political act: it must
therefore be met by political action.

Such as tailing the man to where he would hide and
then having Malcolmson shoot him first. Any questions? But of course there were. He'd have his weapon
by then, could be taken with it, and there'd be half
a dozen charges which fitted. Perhaps, but those
charges would have to be tried. There'd be publicity
however it went and publicity was their enemies' object. They couldn't concede them that by default. But
a dead national of this potent State, one found armed
for a purpose both sides would deplore ...

That would go to the very highest level, the level
where you could fix things quietly. No reporters, no
judges, no tiresome diplomats. Just a van in the night
and a nameless grave. Then mutual relief and some
wicked Martinis.

John looked at his watch: seven minutes had gone.
The muzzle of the other rifle was still visible when he

used the telescope.

He wondered whether old grey Sir James had known about Peggy; he probably had. He knew most things about what concerned him so he'd know that Peggy and John had been friendly, but just how friendly even he might not know. There'd been that week in Paris, another in Rome. John Malcolmson sighed but was unresentful. It hadn't really been on, not Peggy Bannister. He was a part-time assassin, though she didn't know that; all she knew was that he worked in a bank, not the right sort of bank like an old merchant house but a clearing bank with a branch in most High Streets. Peggy Bannister hadn't cared a damn but her parents would have cared intensely. They were that sort of people and dauntingly grand. Would she have married him? John didn't know. He had never quite brought himself to chance it, to expose her to the rows and the strain. God damn Peggy's parents and all that they stood for.

So when His Nibs had shown a ducal interest the pressure on her had been irresistible. Such a match would be a social triumph but also, John suspected, disaster. Nevertheless he had never blamed her. She was the nicest girl but she wasn't his sort, and he'd known that if she tired of him she'd have nowhere to go but to crawl back home. He wouldn't risk that for he'd liked her too well. He killed men for money but he liked to kill cleanly.

His radio came to life again and this time the scout was abridging the rubric. He said in plain English :

'Another delay.'

'What the hell has gone wrong?' John was feeling the tension.

'Some clowns in the crowd running out with banners.'

'What did they say?'

'They said "QUIT VIETNAM".'

'Not much to do with the new town hall. I thought that His Nibs was here to open it.'

Malcolmson had spoken lightly but his Control reacted with sullen anger. 'Men with long hair and girls in tight jeans. They ought to put them into labour camps.'

John switched the set off and went back to waiting. There wasn't any point in commenting. His scout worked at a desk, an establishment man, and he was utterly and grimly committed. John knew that he didn't work for the money, he had more than enough of that already; he served because it released his hatreds, his loathing of what he called subversion. This incident had been *lèse majesté*, at any rate by implication. No decent sound man who played good class club cricket would walk around with impertinent banners.

John stretched on his mattress – the strain was mounting. He was telling himself, though without conviction, that a couple of unexpected delays in no way affected the basic plan and far less his power to carry it out. That was logical but it didn't bite: something was going to go wrong. He sensed it. And of all the colleagues he'd ever worked with he liked and trusted this scout the least. Naturally if something went badly awry he'd be utterly without protection, disowned and left to fend for himself. That was part of the game he'd elected to play, so much so that when he'd talked to Sir James the old man hadn't bothered to state again what was known to both and freely accepted. But there was a distinction and an important one between disowning an agent who'd failed in his mission and letting a colleague down in a crisis. John Malcolmson's scout, who preferred 'Control', was a man for whom he felt reservations.

He sighed again; he was far from happy. If anything went wrong that was bad: it was worse that Peggy might also be caught in it. He could only hope it was still going well for her.

In fact it was going extremely badly. To begin with she'd had to sober up Alfred, a chore which she had never relished. He wasn't a proper alcoholic and sometimes she found she wished he were. He would drink for months, then go dry as a bone, something no true alcoholic could do, and in the intervals while he sweated it out he would try to make love to Peggy *née* Bannister. He made love like an old, old man – it was horrible. Happily this happened seldom: for forty-six weeks of the fifty-two he was as tight as a fart and about as malodorous.

And he'd kicked like a mule at coming at all; he resented all forms of public duty. But cousin Clement had crashed in his car again, a feat he achieved quite depressingly often, and there wasn't another Personage free. Peggy had finally shamed him to action – after all, the State subsidised both of them generously – but that morning he'd been at the bottle again and she'd worked for two hours just to make him presentable. Not, she was thinking, that she'd wholly succeeded. He could get through his lines without falling down but his manner was a long way from gracious. He was sitting with her in the back of the car, and since the weather was fine the car was open. He sat slumped and morose, occasionally muttering. Peggy noticed that the crowd was thin, and what there was was plainly indifferent. They'd had hopes of a Much Greater Person and she and this whisky-sodden duke were a very poor second best indeed.

Nevertheless she smiled and waved bravely. The

duke didn't smile or deign a bow. He had none of the practised bonhomie, condescending perhaps but undeniably charming, which was the hallmark of more professional kinsmen. Peggy looked at her husband again. He frowned rudely. He was a peasant in a full Colonel's uniform.

Margaret, Duchess of Worcester, smiled wryly. She was thinking about a man called Malcolmson whom she'd loved in her way and allowed to go. Not that he'd ever asked her to marry him but that was a shameless self-justification. She knew he'd been near to doing so twice and each time she'd expertly headed him off. . . . Oh yes, she could pile up the snags indefinitely, like Twickenham on a wet winter Saturday, the incomprehensible game which astonishd her, the warm beer in pints drunk with men in club ties. The semi-detached in a sober suburb, and daddy and mummy outraged and resentful. . . .

Until, of course, the grandchildren came. Then they'd come round, they always did. She looked at the man by her side with loathing. He was only in his late forties but she doubted he'd ever give her children.

The ADC was sitting in front and she heard him speak to the driver softly. It sounded like 'Better hurry it up' and the duchess had rather expected the order. She hadn't looked for a triumphal progress but these pavements half-filled with a cool indifference were more unnerving than any demonstration. The men with the banners had not distressed her, she thought them every bit as foolish as John Malcolmson's scout had thought them subversive, and in any case there was less than a furlong before they reached the town hall and official reception. She could feel that the car was moving faster, nearly fifteen miles an hour, she guessed, an unheard of pace for a formal progress. In fact it was doing nearer twenty when the girl ran out and they hit her squarely.

For a moment Peggy thought they'd killed her, but the driver had trodden on powerful brakes. All four in the car had jerked forward roughly and now three of them were straightening out. The duke had slipped down on the floor and was swearing, the girl lay across the bonnet, clawing. She didn't appear to be badly hurt but either she was drunk or drugged. She was bawling incoherently, a stream of abuse interspersed with slogans. Free Peter MacLintock. (Who was MacLintock?) Death to the Rhodesian fascists.

Two plainclothes men had run out from the pavement but a man from the opposite side beat them to it. He leant over into the car and spat.

'Bastards,' he said. 'You privileged bastards.' He had made no attempt to help the girl.

The first and last Duke of Worcester had picked himself off the floor in a fury. He used a handkerchief to dry the spittle. The man spat again and the duke stood up. Peggy could see he had closed a fist. He couldn't dent a pat of butter but the pictures would go round the world.

'No,' she said sharply. She held his arm.

He shook her off and she stood up too. The watcher in the rubble saw her. He saw her but a split second too late.

Jeff Lavazzari lay quiet in the rubble. Unlike Malcolmson he was working alone with no scout in the crowd to tell him by radio that the car and its escort had been delayed. Even if he had known the fact it wouldn't have caused him a moment's worry. He was here, in position, and very well hidden. If he worried there was another reason, for it had all been almost alarmingly easy, this block of unfinished flats, now deserted, the builders' debris on the inviting roof. Nobody had challenged him, and the men who had been shadowing him from the moment he had stepped from his aircraft had been professionals of the highest class. He hadn't seen a thing suspicious – certainly not John Malcolmson behind the innocent-looking curtains opposite. He looked round the other roofs: they were empty. In his own country they'd have been stiff with armed men.

He was an American of Italian blood and could still speak his grandparents' language fluently. Still a Latin at heart he despised all Celts and had very nearly refused the job. What a rabble of bumbling yokels they were! Jeff Lavazzari would have agreed with Sir James. They could fire single shots at sitting targets or brown at a patrol of soldiers, but a single sure shot at a moving target and they had to recruit a Jeff Lavazzari. Even if they had owned a marksman, one of a class they could really rely on, the English police would have picked him up. Such a man wouldn't booze, couldn't pass as a labourer. As for the others, Jeff considered them murderers, misguided and often messy terrorists. His business was killing for money, not politics.

Besides, all political killings were profitless. One killed to control a territory, to sell drugs in it or run the brothels. But that would come after you'd fixed the politics – his race had realised that years ago. Other peoples would try to make money in trade and then, if successful, they'd take to politics. Americans of Italian blood had long since seen that was rather clumsy. Instead they had captured the politics first and the trades had followed behind them naturally. Since not all of these had been orthodox trades and the men who ran them far from conventional a killing or two had been sometimes necessary, but a killing in anger or spite was childish and a killing because of an ancient frustration was worse than just childish, was self-defeating. Only the money had finally tempted him. It had been very good money indeed. He had fallen.

He would have liked to smoke but didn't dare to; he mustn't push his luck too far. Instead he looked down at the street and nodded. It would be a perfectly straightforward shot. It wasn't raining so the car would be open. He had made that a formal term of the contract. If the car was closed the job was off. He wouldn't blind into a closed car and hope, that was work for the barbarous hoodlums who'd hired him. As it was the car would be moving, but slowly, and he was well above the scattered spectators. A single clear sighting was all he asked for, and as he'd placed himself he would have that perfectly. He looked at his rifle, allowing a smile. John Malcolmson could just see the muzzle but Jeff Lavazzari was showing no more. He wouldn't risk showing more, he didn't need to. Not yet, that is, but later he'd have to. He'd no room to move back so the gun must come forward. That wouldn't matter, he had planned his retreat. He'd simply wipe the rifle for fingerprints and leave the police to find it later. In the street below there'd be utter confusion and there was scaffolding at the back of the building. Moreover he had a bowler hat which in England was not what gunmen wore. He'd have an excellent chance once he reached the street and an air passage was booked already.

So he looked at the rifle and smiled affectionately, though affection had not been his first emotion. Sir James had been right, it had been brought in separ-

ately, by a sporting-looking gentleman with a great
many fishing rods in covers. But when Lavazzari had
seen it first he had almost decided to drop the job. He
had expected something much more contemporary, say
a seven-six-two modern FAL with standard NATO
ammunition. A twenty-round magazine perhaps,
though he'd only been needing a single shot. Instead
he'd been given this Mannlicher and his first thought
had been that they'd robbed a museum. But he was a
craftsman who could appreciate craftsmanship and
gradually, if reluctantly, he had fallen in love with the
weapon's sheer beauty. They didn't make things like
this today. It had the characteristic flat-folding bolt
with the safety catch stuck on the end which you
twisted, the sight had a vaguely French-sounding
name, and beautiful highly polished wood ran in elegant curves from the stock to the muzzle. Jeff Lavazzari
fondled it happily. It might be anything up to forty
years old but he realised he'd been paid a compliment.
No competent killer could miss with this one.

Especially when the car stopped dead directly under
where he was hiding, especially when his target stood
up. He put the Mannlicher-Schoenauer to his shoulder,
for the first time showing more than the muzzle, and
he'd been moving into the second pressure when the
girl in the car had stood up too. Committed to fire he
had fired. But he swore.

He never completed the oath. He was dead.

When the car had stopped in front of him Lavazzari
had scarcely believed his luck but John Malcolmson
had been thrown off stride. His business was watching
a rifle's muzzle and the instant it moved to shoot and
kill first; he hadn't expected an uproar below him and
for a second he withdrew his eyes. What they saw was

a girl standing up, then collapsing. He moved them back to his telescope sight, and the splinters from the first shot he fired broke Jeff Lavazzari's back in three places.

John put down the rifle, frozen in fury. The radio had come in again and his scout had begun to yammer senselessly.

'Did you get him all right?'

John Malcolmson neither heard nor answered.

'Control to Polly. Acknowledge at once.'

He was watching the scene in the street below, telling himself he was still deciding, though beneath conscious thought he'd already done so. A crowd was milling around the car and policemen were trying to force their way through it. The other girl had been pulled from the bonnet – John didn't give a thought to her. The ADC had his head in his hands. In no possible sense had he been to blame but he knew about the army. . . . Finished. Two men were lifting Peggy gently but His Nibs hadn't moved from his seat to help them. If he had he'd have lived a few years longer. His arrogant indifference killed him.

The radio said: 'I'm coming over,' and this time John Malcolmson answered sharply.

'Mind your own business.'

'You're under my orders.'

'You know what to do with your orders.'

'Stand fast.'

'Very well,' John said. 'I'll stay here. I'd meant to.'

He could see a man detach himself from the press around the still stationary car. He was nearer to him than John had expected, and he began to run towards the flat. He was a very frightened man indeed for his nature was to mistrust part-timers and he'd heard gossip about John and Peggy.

When he used his key and came in John said nothing. He was lying on the mattress still with a bead on His Grace of Worcester's heart. The reason he hadn't fired was simple: there was a St John's man with his back in the way. His bullets would smash a body to pieces but they wouldn't go through it and kill another. Besides, he wasn't a murderer. No. But shooting that pig in the car wasn't murder. The other man would have got him anyway for John had taken his eye off his muzzle. Peggy had died instead. Intolerable. Above all things it offended justice. Justice now grew from John Malcolmson's rifle.

He wasn't concerned at his scout's arrival: he was a desk man and wouldn't dare interfere, he'd write Minutes but he'd never act.

The opinion was in principle sound but John had misjudged the goad of fear – fear and the desk man's secret compulsion to use violence if he could do so safely. His Control had taken it in at once, the rifle pointing down to the street, its owner tense and intent and waiting. If Malcolmson shot – *when* Malcolmson shot – his organisation would be in serious trouble.

He was carrying a cosh and drew it. Malcomson was lying, defenceless, but Control was a fatal second too late. The shot went away as his cosh came down and the first duke was also the last and the least.

When John Malcolmson woke he was stiff and cold. He felt as though he'd been drugged. He had. On the beach was a pair of parallel tracks, a light aircraft's, he thought, as his senses came back to him. There were notices in a foreign language, oleanders which backed the sand and oil on it. Well, he hadn't expected a cell in a police station. They would never face that since they'd never have dared to. Round his neck was a waterproof bag. He opened it. There was a passport with his photograph but the name of a man he'd never heard of and five thousand pounds in English money.

He picked himself up and began to walk. He didn't blame them, he'd always been wholly expendable. Moreover he had been hired and had failed, indeed he had grossly perverted his orders.

It was generous to have left him some money.

A QUESTION OF CONFIDENCE

by Michael Innes

Bobby Appleby (successful scrum-half retired, and author of that notable anti-novel *The Lumber Room*) had been down from Oxford for a couple of years. But he went back from time to time, sometimes for the day and sometimes on a week-end basis. He had a number of clever friends there who were now busily engaged in digging in for life. They had become, that is to say, junior dons of one or another more or less probationary sort, and had thereby risen from the austerities of undergraduate living to the fleshpots and the thrice-driven beds of down associated with Senior Common Rooms and High Tables. They liked entertaining Bobby, to whom *The Lumber Room* rather than his athletic prowess lent, in their circle, a certain prestige. One of these youths was a historian called Brian Button.

Button sometimes came home with Bobby to Long Dream. Sir John Appleby (policeman retired) rather liked this acquaintance of his son's, and was even accustomed to address him as B.B. – this seemingly with some elderly facetious reference to the deceased art historian Bernhard Berenson. Bobby's B.B. (unlike the real B.B.) came from Yorkshire, a region of which Bobby's father approved. So Appleby was quite pleased when, chancing to look up from his writing-table on a sunny Saturday morning, he saw Bobby's ancient Porsche stationary on the drive, with Bobby climbing out of the driver's seat and B.B. out of the other. But the young men were unprovided with suitcases, which was odd. The young men bolted for the front door as if through a thunder-storm, which was odder still. And seconds later – what was oddest of all – the young men burst without ceremony into the room.

'Daddy!' the distinguished novelist exclaimed – and he seemed positively out of breath – 'here's an awful thing happened. Brian's got mixed up in a murder.'

'Both of you sit down.' Appleby looked with considerably more interest at Mr Button than at his son. B.B. too was out of breath. But B.B. was also as pale as death. The lad – Appleby said to himself – is clean out of his comfortable academic depth. 'And might it be described' – Appleby asked aloud – 'as a particularly gruesome murder?'

'Moderately,' Bobby replied judiciously. 'You see —'

'In Oxford?'

'Yes, of course. We've driven straight over. And you've damn well got to come and clear it up.'

'But, Bobby, it isn't my business to clear up homicides in Oxford: not even in the interest of B.B. Of course, I can be told about it.'

'Well, it seems to have been like this —'

'By B.B. himself, please. It will do him good. So do you go and fetch us drinks. And, Brian, go ahead.'

'Thank you, sir – thank you very much.' Mr Button clearly liked being called Brian for a change; it braced him. 'Perhaps you know the job I've been given. It's ordering and cataloguing the Cannongate Papers.'

'The Third Marquis's stuff?'

'Yes. I'm the Cannongate Lecturer.'

'You lecture on the Papers?'

'Of course not.' B.B. found this a foolish question. 'That's just what I'm called, since I've got to be called something. I get the whole bloody archive in order, and then it's to be edited and published in a grand way, and I shall be Number Two on the job. Quite a thing for me.'

'I'm delighted to hear it. Go on.'

'All Lord Cannongate's papers have been deposited with the college by the trustees. Masses and masses of them – and some of them as confidential as hell.'

'State papers, do you mean?'

'Well yes – but that's not exactly the rub. There's a certain amount of purely personal and family stuff. It hasn't been sieved out. I have to segregate it and lock it up. It has nothing to do with what can ever be published.'

'Then the trustees ought to have done that job themselves.'

'I couldn't agree more. But they're lazy bastards, and the responsibility has come on me. It's a question of confidence. If there's a leak, what follows is a complete shambles, so far as my career's concerned.'

'I see.' Appleby looked with decent sympathy at this agitated young man. 'But I think something has been said about murder? That sounds rather a different order of thing.'

'Yes, of course.' B.B. passed a hand across his brow. 'A sense of proportion, and all that. I must try to get it right.' B.B. took a big breath. 'So just listen.'

And B.B. began to tell his story.

He worked, it seemed, in a kind of commodious dungeon beneath the college library. The cavernous chamber was impregnable; so, within it, were the numerous steel filing cabinets in which the Cannongate Papers had arrived. B.B., coming and going, had only to deal faithfully with locks and keys, and nothing could go wrong. Unfortunately it is not easy, when living in a residential university, to bear at all constantly in mind that the world is inhabited by others as well as scholars and gentlemen, ancient faithful menservants of a quasi-hereditary sort, a few pretty secretaries and an excellent *chef*. One may differ sharply from one's colleagues over such issues as the problem of the historical Socrates; one may even be conscious that at times quite naked and shocking animosities can generate themselves out of less learned matters – as, for example, where to hang a picture or who shall look after the wine; but one doesn't – one simply doesn't – expect to have one's pocket picked or one's researches plagiarised. The concept of the felonious, in short, is one to which it is difficult to give serious thought.

These considerations – or something like them – B.B. did a little divagate to advance, as the early stages of his narrative now unfolded themselves. He had not always been too careful about those bloody keys, and he would look a pretty fool in a witness-box if this ghastly affair had the consequence of depositing him in one before a judge and jury.

Appleby's benevolent reception of the troubles of Bobby's friend didn't stand up to all this too well. He had a simple professional persuasion that keys exist to be turned in locks without fail at appropriate times, and that a young man who has gone vague on instructions he has received and accepted in such a matter ought not to be let off being told that he has been improperly negligent. On the other hand it was possible that B.B. was himself feeling very bad indeed. These were considerations that required balanced utterance.

'I hope,' Appleby said, 'that we needn't conclude your culpable carelessness over these things to have been the direct occasion of somebody's getting murdered. It sounds inherently improbable. But go on.'

'Well, sir, there's rather a difficult one there.' B.B. was recovering from the extreme disarray in which he had arrived at Dream. 'I suppose the original chunk of dirty work – a bit of thieving – couldn't have happened if I'd always been right on the ball over those rotten keys. But the murder's a different matter. That seems to have been the result of my having, as a matter of fact, a brighter moment.'

'Brian saw the significance of the electricity.' Bobby Appleby, who had returned to his father's study deftly carrying a decanter, three glasses and a plate of chocolate biscuits, offered this luminous remark. 'Absolutely top-detective stuff, if you ask me.'

'But I don't ask you. So just pour us that sherry and be quiet.' Appleby turned back to Mr Button. 'More about your brighter moment, please.'

'When I happen on any paper dealing with a certain delicate and purely family matter, I have instructions to photocopy it. There's some prospect of a law-suit, it seems, over whether a grandson of *my* Lord Cannongate was of legitimate birth or not; and a sort of dossier has to be got together for some solicitors.'

'You have to make only one copy?'

'Yes – and when I came on something relevant earlier this week I did just that. We have a machine on which we can do the job ourselves, you see, in one of the college offices. There were eight pages of the stuff, and when I'd made a copy I filed the eight sheets of it away in a special box with other photocopies of similar material. That was on Monday. Yesterday morning I had to go to that box again, and I happened to turn over those particular copies. Only, the sheets were pretty well stuck to each other still. So you see.'

'No, Brian, I *don't* see.' Appleby glanced from the Cannongate Lecturer to the creator of *The Lumber*

Room (who was punishing the chocolate biscuits rather more heavily than the sherry). He might have been wondering whether England was exclusively populated by excessively clever young men. 'Why should they be stuck to each other?'

'Because of what Bobby says – the electricity.' B.B. seemed surprised that this had not been immediately apparent. 'Those photocopying machines are uncommonly lavish with it. Static electricity, I think it's called. If you stack your copies one on top of another as they come out of the contraption, they cling to one another like —'

'Like characters in a skin-flick.' Bobby had momentarily stopped munching to offer this helpful simile. 'And that's what Brian found.'

'I see.' Appleby was no longer mystified. 'The electrical phenomenon fades, and therefore the sheets manifesting it yesterday could not be those which you had filed away on Monday. Earlier yesterday, or just a little before that, somebody had extracted your copies from their box; photocopied them in turn; and then – inadvertently, perhaps – returned to the box not the older copies but the newer ones. And, but for this curious electrical or magnetic effect on the paper, and but for your being alert enough to notice it and draw the necessary inference, nobody need ever have known that there had been any monkey-business at all.'

'That's it, sir. And, if I may say so, pretty hot of you to get there in one.'

'Thank you very much,' Appleby said a shade grimly. 'It doesn't exactly tax the intellect. And just what did you do, Brian, when you made this unfortunate discovery?'

'I went straight to our Master, Robert Durham, and told him the whole thing. There was nothing else for it but to confess to the head man.'

'That was thoroughly sensible of you.' Appleby spoke as a man mollified. 'And how has the Master taken it?'

'How *did* he take it,' Bobby corrected, and reached for another biscuit.

'*What?*' Appleby looked from one to the other young man aghast. 'Brian . . .?'

'Yes, sir. You see, the Master seemed to have ideas about what had happened, although he didn't tell me what they were. It appeared to ring a bell. And that must be why they've murdered him.'

'Good God!' Appleby had a passing acquaintance with the scholar thus summarily disposed of.

'We could have better spared a better man.' Bobby offered this improving quotation with some solemnity. 'Of course, the old boy had had his life. I did feel that. He must have been sixty, if he was a day. He'd toasted his bottom before the fire of life. It sank —'

'Possibly so.' Appleby made no attempt to find this out-of-turn mortuary humour diverting, but he did perhaps judge it, from Bobby, a shade mysterious.

'Still,' Bobby went on, 'even if the Master was a clear case for euthanasia, the thing must be cleared up. *You* must come and clear it up, as I've said. The fact is, they may be getting round to imagining things.'

'Who do you mean by "they"? B.B. seems to be applying the word to a gang of assassins.'

'What *I* mean is the police.' Bobby Appleby was suddenly speaking slowly and carefully. 'They may pitch on some quite unsuitable suspect. For instance, on B.B. himself. You see, there are one or two things you haven't yet heard.'

'To my confusion, Bobby means.' Mr Button, who had cheered up while retailing his acumen over the electrified photocopies, was again sunk in gloom, and he had blurted this out after a short expressive silence. 'I think the police believe I took the Master a cock-and-bull story, just as a cover-up for something else. I think they believe the Master spotted my deception, and that I killed him because otherwise I'd have been turfed out in disgrace and it would have been the end of me.'

'That's a succinct statement, at least.' Appleby was looking at his son's friend gravely. 'Does it mean that, in addition to being careless with those keys, you had been at fault in some other way as well?'

'I'm afraid it does. You see, I'd had the idea of writing a few popular articles on the side.'

'My dear young man! You were going to publicise this intimate Cannongate family scandal you've been talking about?'

'Of course not.' B.B. had flushed darkly. 'Just some purely political things. I'd have got permission, and all that, from the trustees. But I felt I wanted to have a definite proposition to put to them. So I had a news-paper chap up from London several times, and showed him this and that. It was a bit irregular, I suppose. It could have looked bad. As a matter of fact, our senior History Tutor came on us a couple of times, and didn't seem to like it. I expect he has told the pigs.'

'As it had undoubtedly now become his duty to do.' Appleby wasn't pleased by this manner of referring to the police. 'But this London contact of yours could at least substantiate your comparatively blameless inten-tions?'

'I suppose so.'

'On the other hand, if this journalist is an unscrupu-lous person, might he have come back into the college and done this thieving and copying himself? Had you told him about those more intimate papers? Even shown them to him?'

'Not shown them. And only mentioned them in a general way. A bit of talk over a pint. He may have gathered where they were kept.'

'Could he, as a stranger, have got swiftly at the photocopying machine?'

'Well, yes – in theory. I took him in there and copied something trivial for him – just to show him we're quite up to date. It's all a bit unfortunate.'

'I agree. And is there anything else that's unfortunate? For example, have you done any other indiscreet talking about this scandal-department in the Cannongate Papers?'

'No, of course not. Or only to Bruno.'

'Very well, B.B. Tell me about Bruno.'

'Bruno Bone is our English Tutor, although he's pretty well just a contemporary of Bobby and me. Teaches Wordsworth and Coleridge and all that sort of stuff. But, really, he wants to be a novelist. More junk yards, so to speak.' This impertinent glance at Bobby's masterpiece was accompanied by rather a joyless laugh on B.B.'s part. 'I told Bruno one evening that there was a whole novel in those damned private papers.'

'That was sheer nonsense, I suppose?'

'I'm afraid so. You know how it is, late at night and after some drinks. Talking for effect, and all that.'

'But at least your brilliant conversation apprised Mr Bone that these scandalous papers exist? Did he take any further interest in them?'

'Well, yes. Bruno came in one morning and asked to have a dekko. He was a bit huffed when I told him it couldn't be done.'

'Just how did you tell him?'

'Oh, I slapped the relevant box and said "Not for you, my boy".'

'I see.' Appleby gazed in some fascination at this unbelievably luckless youth. 'Tell me, B.B. Of course there isn't the material for a novel in your wretched dossier. But might there be material for blackmail?'

'Definitely, I'd say. It's not all exactly past history, you know. There are still people alive —'

'All right – we needn't go into details yet. But tell me this: might the Master have got to know about your chatter to Bruno Bone?'

'It's not unlikely. Bruno's an idiot. Talk about anything to anybody.'

'That's a habit I'm glad to feel you disapprove of. Do you think Bruno could have developed some morbid and irrational curiosity as a result of all this, and have actually abstracted that particular bunch of papers and made copies of them?'

'I suppose it's possible. Those literary characters are wildly neurotic.'

'And the Master might have found it – with the result that Bruno's own career would suddenly have been very much at risk?'

'Yes. The Master is – was – rather a dab at nosing things out.'

'And that brings us to the last relevant point at the moment. Just how did Dr Durham die?'

'Brains blown out.' Bobby Appleby (who had finished the last chocolate biscuit) produced this robustly. 'With some sort of revolver, it seems. Not something it's likely that Brian keeps handy, I'd have thought.'

'Nor Bruno,' B.B. said handsomely.

'Nor any stray blackmailer, either.' Appleby was frowning. 'You wouldn't know whether the police are claiming to have found the weapon?'

'Oh, yes.' Bobby nodded vigorously. 'It was just lying on the carpet in the Master's study.'

'That's where I'd expect it to be.' Appleby sounded faintly puzzled. 'You know, the great majority of men who are found with their brains blown out have effected the messy job themselves. And even in the moment of death some spasm or convulsion can result in the weapon's landing yards away. So, just for the moment, this story of yours sounds to me something of a mare's nest. Robert Durham is in some pathological state of depression and suddenly makes away with himself. And then in comes Brian's bad conscience about his handling of his archive. Bobby, wouldn't you agree? You've said something that makes me think you would agree.'

'Have I?' Bobby seemed not to make much of this. 'Durham wasn't *my* Master, you know. He got the job only when mine died a couple of years ago. But I've seen enough of him to know that he was a rum bird.'

'Secretive,' B.B. added. 'Nobody quite knew what he was up to. He was a bit remote. Brooding type. And a sick man, some said.'

'God bless my soul!' As he made use of this antique expression, Sir John Appleby got to his feet. 'Unless you're both having me up the garden path, you're describing a thoroughly persuasive candidate for suicide. Not that such don't get murdered from time to time. They may ingeniously elect liquidation in one way or another, without so much as being conscious of the fact. Which is psychologically interesting, no doubt, but murder it nevertheless remains.' Appleby paused, and looked searchingly from one young man to the other. 'Is there anything else I ought to know?'

'Not in the way of fact, I'd say.' For the moment, Bobby Appleby (so childishly addicted to chocolate biscuits) appeared to have taken charge of things. 'Of course, the people who may have extra facts are the police. And they *do* have something. I don't know what – but I know it's there. I was present when they talked to Brian early this morning. They kept mum, but I knew they had *something*.' Bobby grinned at his father. 'Family instinct, perhaps. It's why I brought Brian over to Dream. You *can* take a hand?'

'I can stroll around the college, and have a chat here and there. I'd tell the Chief Constable, and he wouldn't mind a bit – always provided I was tactful with his men on the spot. And being *that* is one of the things I keep a grip on even in senescence.' Appleby, as he momentarily adopted this humorous vein, let his glance stray out of the window. It fixed itself briefly, and then returned to the two young men. 'I'll make a call or two,' he said easily, and moved towards the door. 'Drink up the sherry meanwhile: there's about a thimbleful left for each of you.'

With this, Appleby left the room. But he was back before much in the way of telephone-calls could have been achieved.

'We were talking about the police,' he said gently. 'As a matter of fact, they're here; and – Brian – they very probably have a warrant for your arrest.'

'The personalities of the people concerned?' The Vice-Master, who was called Fordyce, looked at Appleby doubtfully. 'That's not what the local police are asking. They want to know who had keys to what, and when who could have been where.'

'Quite right. Absolutely essential.' Appleby nodded approvingly. 'It's what gets the results – in nine cases

out of ten. And, on this occasion, they appear to have
got a result quite rapidly. Too rapidly, I think you'd
say?'

'Of course I'd say. The notion of that young man
Brian Button providing himself with a revolver and
shooting the Master dead with it in his own study is
simply too fantastic to stand up.'

'But just at the moment, Vice-Master, it seems to
be standing up rather well. The police have no doubt
about what Dr Durham was doing when he was shot
down – and it's what they've discovered that has led
them to question our young man. Durham was dictating a letter on his tape-recorder for his secretary to
type out later. It was to the Cannongate trustees, and
said flatly that Button had been guilty of professional
misconduct of so scandalous a sort that he must be dismissed at once – even although it meant that all academic employment would henceforth be closed to
him.'

'It was a very strange thing for the Master to propose
to write, Sir John.'

'Well, there it is. The tape isn't to be denied. The
Master appears to have flicked the switch that stops the
machine simply because he was interrupted while on
the job. So the record remained for the police to find.'

'I understand the police case. Button has admitted
going to see the Master early yesterday morning and
telling him a story about rifled papers. It is now supposed that he returned again in the late afternoon,
armed and resolved. The Master told him of the step
he proposed to take, but without saying that he had at
that moment broken off from recording his letter. So
Button killed him, hoping thus to smother up the whole
thing. I repeat that it is utter nonsense, completely

alien to Brian Button's character, such as it is. A somewhat irresponsible young man, perhaps. But not precisely bloody, bold and resolute.'

'It's Durham's character that interests me more. And
aren't you saying that he too seems to have behaved *out*
of character?'

'In a sense, that is so.' Fordyce had taken this point
soberly. 'But perhaps I have to say that, although I
knew Robert Durham long before he became Master,
I never quite understood the man. I have sometimes
thought of him as harbouring that degree of inner
instability which is liable to produce what they call a
personality-change. And yet that is a fantastic speculation.'

'At least a change of job, one supposes, may bring out
something roughly of that sort. Was there any particular regard in which he appeared to you to be
changing?'

'I can scarcely answer that without appearing very
much at sea, Sir John. In one aspect Durham was a
man growing detached, remote, fatigued. In another,
he was becoming irascible, authoritarian and increasingly prone to flashes of odd behaviour. He could behave like an old-fashioned headmaster with a vindictive
turn of mind.'

'Dear me! That sort of thing surely doesn't cut
much ice with undergraduates today?'

'Decidedly not. They can be a very great nuisance,
our young men. But it is reason alone that is of any
avail with them. It's something they have a little begun
to get the hang of. Talk sense patiently enough and
without condescension – and round they always come.'
Fordyce had delivered this high doctrine with an effect
of sudden intellectual conviction. 'Durham had lost
grip on that.'

'How did he get along with the younger dons?'

'Ah! Not too well.'

'To the extent of anything like feud? With Button himself, for instance?'

'With Button, I'd scarcely suppose so – although the lad may have annoyed him. Nor with any of them to what you might call a point of naked animosity. Bone might be an exception.'

'Bone? A young man called Bruno Bone?'

'Yes. I'm not sure that Bone, for whatever reason, hadn't got to the point of hating Durham in his guts.' It was rather unexpectedly that the Vice-Master had produced this strong expression.

'But Bone, too, would scarcely be bloody, bold and resolute?'

'Of course not. He —' The Vice-Master, who seemed to have produced this reply by rote, suddenly checked himself. 'Do you know,' he said, 'that I wouldn't be quite confident of that? But then I'm coming to wonder what I shall ever be robustly confident about again. This is an undermining affair, Sir John.'

Bruno Bone, a lanky, prematurely bald young man, was spending his Saturday afternoon banging away on his typewriter. Perhaps he was writing a lecture, or perhaps he was writing a novel. Whichever it was, he didn't seem much to care for being interrupted by the mere father of the author of *The Lumber Room*.

'Yes, of course I know they've arrested Button,' Bone said. 'So what?'

'I'd rather suppose you might be distressed or concerned. Not that they have, perhaps, quite arrested him. He's helping them with their inquiries. They have to tread carefully, you know. But it's true they hold a document from a magistrate. It's in reserve. But

I'd simply like to ask, Mr Bone, what you think of the affair.'

'Absolute poppycock. Brian Button's an irresponsible idiot, and I wouldn't trust him with looking after the beer in the buttery, let alone those Cannongate Papers. But he wouldn't shoot old bloody Durham. Wouldn't have the nerve.'

'Would you?'

'If you weren't old enough to be my father, I'd tell you that was a damned impertinent question.'

'Never mind the impertinence. Would you?'

'I don't know that I know.' Bruno Bone was of a sudden entirely amenable. 'It's an interesting speculation. On the whole – I'm ashamed to say – I guess not.'

'Or would anybody else in the college?'

'Can't think of anybody.'

'Then I'm left – so far as anybody who has been put a name to goes – with a London journalist whom Button sent for and talked to a shade rashly. There are journalists, I suppose, who are fit for anything.'

'This one may have scented a hopeful whiff of blackmail, or something of that kind? And the Master may have got on to what he was up to, and had his brains blown out for his pains? I wouldn't like to have to render such a course of events plausible in a novel.'

'If you ever try, I'll hope to read your attempt at it.' Appleby gave this quite a handsome sound. 'When did you last see Dr Durham?'

'When did I last see my father?' Bruno Bone was amused. 'Quite late in the day, really. I'm not a bad suspect, come to think of it. Smart of you to be chasing me up, Sir John. Quite Bobby's father, if I may say so. Bobby's bright.'

'I never judged him exactly dim – but the point's

not of the first relevance. Be more precise, please.'

'Very well. I went to see the old brute about an hour before he was indubitably dead. Probably the last man in, so to speak. A breathless hush in the close, and all that. I wanted to sound him out about the prospects of my touching the college for a travel grant. California. Awful universities, but a marvellous climate. Durham treated me as if I was a ghost. Bizarre, wouldn't you say? Considering he was so well on the way to becoming one himself.'

'No doubt. What was the Master doing?'

'Concocting a letter.'

'On some sort of dictaphone?'

'Nothing of the sort. Laborious pen and ink. And putting a lot of concentration into it, I'd say. He made a civil pretence of listening to me for about thirty seconds, and then turfed me out. He was back on his job before I'd reached the door.'

'And that was the last you saw of him?'

'No, it wasn't.' Bruno Bone was sardonically triumphant. 'And here's where I get off the hook. I saw him ten minutes later – and so must plenty of other people – crossing the great quadrangle, with his letter in his hand. He went out through the main gate, crossed the road to the post office, shoved his letter into the box and came back.'

'There would be nothing particularly out of the way, would there, about all that?'

'Of course there would. He had only to leave the thing on a table in his hall, and it would have been collected and dealt with by a college messenger.'

'Thank you very much, Mr Bone. And I apologise for disturbing you.'

Appleby's final call was on the senior History Tutor,

an elderly man called Farnaby. Farnaby, he supposed, was in some vague and informal fashion Brian Button's boss.

'One of Button's indiscretions,' Appleby said, 'appears to have been dreaming up some popular articles based on the documents in his charge, and calling in a man from some paper or other with whom to discuss the matter. Would you term his doing that a grave breach of confidence?'

'Certainly not. Button ought, no doubt, to have mentioned the proposal to the Master or to myself in the first instance. It might even be said that there was a slight element of discourtesy in his conduct of the matter; and anything of the kind is, of course, greatly to be deprecated in a society like ours.'

'Of course.'

'But let us simply call it an error of judgement. Button has the makings of a complete scholar; but of what may be called *practical* judgement he has very little sense.'

'I see. Would you say, Mr Farnaby, that the young man's lack of practical judgement might extend to his supposing it judicious to murder Dr Durham?'

'Of course not. I am almost inclined, Sir John, to say that the question could be asked only in a frivolous spirit. It is utter nonsense.'

'So everybody except the police appears to feel. Might Button be described as a protege of yours?'

'I don't think we go in for proteges.' Farnaby had frowned. 'But I certainly feel in some degree responsible for him. He was my pupil, and it was I who recommended him for his present employment.'

'Thank you. Now, it appears to me, Mr Farnaby, that we have at present just one hard fact in this affair. The day before yesterday, or thereabout, some person

unknown abstracted eight sheets from a file of photocopies, photocopied those photocopies anew and then
returned the newer and not the older photocopies to
the file. The switch was almost certainly fortuitous
rather than intentional. It could not have been designed
to attract Button's attention, since there was no particular likelihood of his turning over those particular
papers again before the static electricity had faded
from them. At this specific point, then, we have no
reason to suspect any sort of plot against the young
man.'

'Clearly not.'

'Button went to the Master and told his story. The
Master – if Button is to be believed, and if he didn't
form a false impression – the Master responded to the
story as if he had some inkling of what lay behind it.
It rang a bell. That is Button's phrase for it. Does that
suggest anything to you?'

'Nothing whatever, I fear.'

'I suppose everybody would have learnt almost at
once about Button's cleverness in tumbling to the im-
plications of that small electrical phenomenon?'

'Almost certainly. He's a young man who can't help
chattering.'

'Do you think that his chatterbox quality, and perhaps other forms of tiresomeness, may have been irri-
tating the Master in a manner, or to a degree, Button
himself wasn't aware of?'

'I'm afraid it is only too probable. Poor Durham was
becoming rather intolerant of folly.'

'That seems to be a view generally held – and it
brings me to my last point. The Vice-Master has given
me some impression of Durham as a man. And he
judges it rather odd, for one thing, that Durham should
have thought to dictate a letter to the Cannongate

trustees that could only have resulted in Button's being sacked. But again – and rather contradictorily – he represents Durham as increasingly irascible, indeed vindictive. How would you yourself describe the man?'

'He owned a certain complexity of character, I suppose. Sit beside him at dinner, and you might judge him rather a dull – even a morose man, particularly during his recent ill-health. But in solitude and at his desk he must have become something quite different, since his writing was often brilliantly witty. And maliciously witty, it may be added; whereas in all his college relations his sense of the academic proprieties extended almost to the rectitudinous.' Farnaby paused, and seemed to become aware of this speech as a shade on the heavy side. 'In fact,' he added, 'poor Robert Durham, barring occasional acts of almost alarming eccentricity, was a bit of a bore. But it would have been a safe bet that the memoirs he was working on would have been highly entertaining. You will recall that he was in political life as a younger man, and knew everybody there was to know. It was probably because he found Oxford a bit of a bore that *we* found *him* one. But I must not speak uncharitably. A horrifying mystery like this is a chastening thing.'

'It is, no doubt, horrifying.' Appleby stood up. 'Or, if not horrifying, at least distressing. Whether it is a mystery is another matter. We can only wait and see.'

'Wait and see, Sir John! I very much hope that the most active steps are being taken to clear the matter up.'

'In a sense, perhaps they are. A little patience is what is required, all the same.'

'And my unfortunate young colleague has to set us an example in the matter?' Farnaby spoke with asperity. 'Button has to rest content in his cell?'

'I think not. It is improbable that any very definitive step has been taken in regard to him. Perhaps I can make myself useful – in this way if in no other, my dear sir – by persuading my former colleagues to part with him. In fact, I'll take him back to Dream with me. He and Bobby can play tennis.'

'And for how long will they have to do *that*?' Although he uttered this question challengingly, Farnaby was clearly much relieved.

'Oh, until Monday morning. It's my guess that between breakfast and lunch on that day Dr Durham's demise will effectively clear itself up.'

And it was at ten o'clock on Monday that Appleby strolled out to the tennis court. A police car had arrived at Dream and departed again, and Appleby now had some papers in his hand.

'Relax,' he said to the two young men. 'Your late Master wilfully sought his own salvation. Or that's how the First Grave Digger would put it. *Felo de se*. The letter has arrived, and all is clear.'

'The letter?' Brian Button repeated. 'The one he was dictating—'

'No, no, B.B. Have some sense, my dear boy. The one your friend Bruno came on him writing, and that he took over to the post office himself. Stamped, of course, as second-class mail.'

'I don't understand you, sir.' B.B. had sat down on a garden seat; he was almost as pale as when he had arrived at Dream in the first instance.

'And I'm blessed if I do either.' Bobby Appleby chucked his tennis racket on the grass at his feet. 'Explain – for goodness sake.'

'Come, come – where's all that absolutely top-detective stuff?' Appleby was in irritatingly good humour. 'And, Bobby, you had an instinct it was all a matter of Durham's calling it a day: don't you remember your prattle about the fire of life, and euthanasia, and whatever? As for the letter, it stared us in the face. The Master didn't want it to go out of his lodging through the college messenger service, so he took it to the post himself.'

'He was anxious,' B.B. demanded, 'to conceal whom he was writing to?'

'Not exactly that. *The letter was to somebody in college.* And he didn't want to risk its being delivered, after his death, more or less straightaway by hand. Despatched by second-class mail, it would be delivered this morning. And it was. To the Vice-Master.'

'And just what was this in aid of?' It was clear from his tone that Brian Button already dimly knew.

'It was in aid, my dear lad, of what his seemingly interrupted communication to the Cannongate trustees on that tape-recorder was also in aid of. Something quite extravagantly malevolent. For let's face it, B.B. You'd annoyed him. You'd annoyed him quite a lot. And he was maliciously resolved to make his departure from this life the occasion of your experiencing *un mauvais quart d'heure*. Or rather more.'

'He thought it was really me who had done that monkeying with the photocopies?'

'No, B.B. He couldn't have thought that. For the Master had done that copying turn himself. Incident-ally, the photocopying machine has been in use this morning. By the police. And they've sent me out this.' Appleby handed a paper to B.B. 'From the Master to the Vice-Master. Robert Durham's testament, poor chap.'

My dear Adrian,

First, let me say how much I hope that the Fellows will elect you into the Mastership. If it should come about that I am permitted to look down upon the college from on high, or obliged to peer up at it from below, this will be the spectacle I shall most wish to view. Bless you, my dear man.

Secondly, pray have the police release that wretched Button. (Is not this appropriately reminiscent of some of the last words of Shakespeare's Lear?) If he be not in custody as you read this, it is because they have been so stupid and negligent as to neglect the tape-recorder on my desk. But surely not even Dogberry and Verges could be so dull.

Button needs a lesson in (as we used to say) pulling his socks up. He is also (what, most illogically, I cannot quite forgive him) the immediate occasion of the step I am about to take. The Cannongate Papers contain some fascinating things, and the censurable carelessness of this young man prompted me to help myself in a clandestine fashion to certain material useful to – shall I say? – an historian of the intimate *mores* of the more elevated classes of society at least not so very long ago. Unfortunately the tiresome Button is very acute; he detected the theft, and came to tell me about it with a mingling of trepidation, uneasiness, complacency and self-congratulation which has extremely offended me.

I need not speak of my present state of health. What has told me that the time has come is really, and precisely, this Button business. He hasn't found me out but *I* have found *myself* out. And in an action of the weirdest eccentricity! As that equally tiresome Bruno Bone would tell you, the poet Pope speaks of Heads of Houses who beastly Skelton quote. But who ever heard of a Head of a House given to petty nocturnal pilferings?

Ave, Hadriane, moriturus te salutat.

ROBERT DURHAM
Master

DEATH IN THE LONG GRASS

by Geoffrey Rose

Think of me if ever you go down to Redemption City.
Especially if you go down at night, as I did, when you
can hardly tell the fireflies from the stars and can't lay
your hand on the horizon.

I'd been put ashore that afternoon. It was an un-
scheduled stop. When I showed the Captain my little
bit of paper he had to comply, but he didn't much like
me or my little bit of paper. We hung about until they'd
raised an immigration official from somewhere – the
grave, by the look of him – and then formalities were
hurried through in the Captain's cabin, where a breeze
fluttered the green curtains. It was tea-time when I
left. The string quartet were playing hit tunes of 1910
while the old women who'd occupied the best arm-
chairs immediately after lunch plied deft fingers among
the cakes. They may not have known which century
they were living in, but they never made a mistake
about feeding-time. They'd heard I was to be put
ashore, and regarded me with furtive contempt or
sympathy as if I'd not paid my fare. The sympathetic
gave me messages for nephews and grandsons who had
'done very well' somewhere in the mysterious interior,
or told me of uncles who'd been killed there by pyg-
mies. They spoke of that continent as one better seen
from off-shore than penetrated. I didn't disbelieve
them, but my little bit of paper was binding on me as
well as on those I showed it to. So I was set on the quay
of a small town – I never knew its name – and the liner
made full steam away, glad to see the last of me. I may

have been a briefly lingering puzzle to the old women as they resumed the novels and knitting which must amuse them through the long hours until dinner.

I was left alone on the quay. The immigration official saw no reason to keep me company. I stood waiting for the motor-car which was to meet me. The air was full of rose-gold light. It coloured the mountains and the sea. The naive might have thought it meant something good was going to happen, but I knew all that would happen was that in a few minutes darkness would fall. The illuminations, then darkness. And if you ask what the illuminations are for, what they celebrate, you're told they celebrate only themselves. And by the time you know that, they're over. So I wasn't expecting anything good. The appearance of my transport fairly soon and no trouble in the meantime would be good enough for me. Men were sitting outside the several cafes, talking intensely but quietly, gesturing often, greeting friends among those who promenaded the quay. Some wore jackets draped on their shoulders, cape fashion. Some walked with arms linked or about each other's neck. There was much embracing and hand-holding when friends met. No women to be seen. Presumably they were penned in the shuttered houses, kept for work and pleasure, while affection was a thing among men. I didn't mind that. What I did mind was that although courtesy kept their eyes averted from a stranger all were aware of me, their consciousness transfixing me as if each had turned and thrown a knife. I've seen plenty of open violence. I can cope with that. I mean you can take your choice, join the fight or run away. But in those languid southern towns there's a covert violence which keeps you shifting from one foot to the other. So I was glad to see the motor-car.

It was dark by that time. I didn't tell the driver he

was late. It would have meant nothing to him. Late and
Early have as little meaning down there as Right and
Wrong. Things just happen. He drove fast and reck-
lessly. I shut my eyes so I shouldn't see when our road
was only a few feet wide between mountain face and
abyss. Dangers I'm not paid for upset me. 'On important business, Boss?' asked the driver. Obviously he
reckoned anybody who had a liner stop there must be
important.

'It's important to me,' I said.

'You come to kill somebody?'

'D'you have much death here?'

'No more than anywhere else. But sooner sometimes.' He grinned and took both hands from the wheel
to light a cigarette, as if demonstrating his point. I
shut my eyes again. We didn't say anything else. There
didn't seem anything else to say. At intervals I opened
my eyes and saw the fireflies and the stars spelling
bright words I didn't know. At last I saw a new brightness – the lights of a city below us. That's a language
I know too well.

We stopped at an hotel and the driver carried my
bag through the revolving door. The entrance hall
was used as a lounge too. Men sat drinking there. They
were better dressed than the men at the quay but had
the same air of latent hostility. Otherwise it was an entrance hall like a hundred others – marble floor, probably imitation, big fan spinning near the ceiling, palms
in pots, those deadly fronds that strangle the life out of
you from Bournemouth to Paraguay. Some of the
drinkers appeared to know my driver. They called to
him in Spanish and he answered. One, a tall man with
an eagle face, approached us. He too wore his jacket
like a cape, and had altogether the manner of an
operatic brigand – a self-conscious swagger, a pointless

bravado. He stopped about a yard from me, arms akimbo, head flung back, and said something in a challenging tone. I asked the driver to translate.

'I tell them you are interested in death. He says death is in the long grass.'

'What does that mean? Is it a local saying?'

The stranger spoke again, very rapidly.

'What now?'

'He says he doesn't want to die in the long grass.'

'Tell him that so far as I'm concerned he doesn't have to.' He appeared to go on saying it, repeating the same words over and over with growing excitement, until two of his companions drew him back to his chair.

'He was a great patriot,' said the driver. 'But he had a bad time in the Revolution, and it left him not quite right.' I looked again at the flightless eagle, thinking him an ill omen for his country and for my mission in it, and continued to the reception desk.

The next morning had no room for gloomy thoughts. The city glittered, an architecture of air and light. In the street, far below my balcony, water-carts were working. Flowers which lined and divided the street caught drops of spray and sparkled like flowers in Paradise.

My first business was with the Chief of Police. I wasn't pleased to recognise him as the brigand of the hotel foyer, the man who was so particular about where he would die. I'd assumed he'd been on the wrong side of the Revolution, but come to think of it those who had weren't likely to be seen much in public. Obviously he'd been given his post as a reward. I don't care for policemen whose minds are affected. I don't care for policemen who sit drinking with the town lay-abouts. I don't care for foreigners who speak English with a more educated accent than I do. And least of all do I care for a man whose eyes are as bleak and anonymous when he takes off his dark glasses as they were before.

'Why didn't you speak English last night?' I asked as he motioned me to a chair.

'It doesn't do to advertise all one's accomplishments.' He read my little bit of paper with a great show of courtesy. The courtesy was in inverse ratio to the help, I reckoned. The ship's Captain had scowled because he must do what I asked. This fellow smiled because he wasn't going to do anything. 'I am at your service,' he said. 'But you must understand our difficulties. In your country the law was made a long time ago. Here it is still on the anvil, and the strongest party wields the hammer.' He enjoyed listening to himself so much that my listening too would have seemed an intrusion. I looked round the room and wondered whether I should be offered a drink, preferably with ice. The blacksmith metaphors went on. Perhaps that was how he had started life. You find some funny ups and downs in those revolutionary countries. I became aware that he'd stopped talking. 'So the long and short of it,' I said, giving him a chance to repeat anything important.

'The long and short of it,' he replied, handing my papers back across the desk, 'is that you have come to the wrong country. You want to extradite a man who has killed somebody and stolen a million of money. Death is so common here and money so scarce that neither crime appears real to the third party.'

'Who's the third party?'

His smile faded. The third party must have got into the act while I wasn't listening.

'The people. Not the law enforcers nor the law breakers, but that third party who determine the effective strength of law. In England the public respect law, so your work is easy. We have no more criminals than you, but our peple despise law, sympathising rather with the man on the run than the man with the warrant.'

'I'd already sensed that,' I said, remembering the loungers on the quay. 'But I'm surprised you call it a poor country. This town looks prosperous enough.'

'We have no money of our own. Foreign governments finance us, pay us to hate each other and sometimes to kill each other. So you see we cannot take seriously the charges against this man.' He tapped the extradition order, which I hadn't yet picked up. 'We shall be very polite, but we shall not really care. What will you drink?'

While he poured it I wondered when his mental unbalance would appear. No sign of it so far. Perhaps it needed a little alcohol, as a cliff-top house which looks safe seen from landward will collapse at the next lick of sea.

'D'you have many English here?'

'All nationalities come here, English among them. I don't know why.' He seemed to include my visit in the riddle.

'My superiors believe this man will come into a city – one, because he'll think himself safer in a crowd, and two, because it's his proper climate.'

'Yes.' I couldn't tell whether he meant Yes that's sound reasoning, or Yes that's the kind of thing one's superiors do think. 'Foreign visitors must surrender their passports and the people with whom they stay must submit details to us. At least that's the regulation. Reputable hotel-keepers observe it. No visitor corresponding with the description and picture you sent us has been reported. But your man might use a false passport. Also there are other hotels which let rooms by the hour, if you understand me.'

'Disorderly houses, we call them.'

'Disorderly houses. That is exquisite. I must remember. A man with plenty of money might stay in such a place and never be asked for his passport. We will make a tour. It will amuse you. And you might find your man.'

'But you doubt it?'

'You have known me long enough to know that I doubt most things.'

'Where would you hide if you were on the run?'

He had risen, and now paused in the act of taking his jacket from the back of his chair. 'I? You are not looking for me.'

'But where would you?'

'I would not come into the city. I would stay outside, in the long grass.'

'Where death is.'

'What?'

'You said last night that death is in the long grass.'

'So it is.' He stood silent a minute before continuing, 'But if I were on the run I would go there. Death is a game two can play, and out there the best man doesn't always win. Let us begin our tour.'

We drove through the city in a big white motor-car, siren wailing. 'Is that necessary?' I asked.

'No, but we must assert ourselves.'

The assertion made no difference. Nobody hurried out of our way, or even turned to look at us. He appeared amused by this universal contempt.

'If my man is in one of these places he'll be up and away when he hears that thing blaring.'

'Don't worry. If the customers jumped up at every police siren they would never do what they come to do.'

We entered an older part of the town – narrower

streets, wrought-iron balconies, coats-of-arms over doors, these elegances partly hidden by washing hung to dry. Beyond a gateway empty of gates I glimpsed a courtyard with a well and a grand flight of stairs leading nowhere, broken in mid-air. We stopped outside one of the houses. 'Business is good,' said my companion, pointing to window boxes full of geraniums. He broke off a cluster and put it in my button-hole, saying, 'We must look a little festive or we shall frighten them.'

A man was sitting at a desk inside, like the receptionist at a pretentious hairdresser's. His rings, watch, tie-pin and a bit of chain round his wrist all glittered in the sunlight. Don't ask me what the chain was. Maybe he'd broken loose from a golden prison. I'm not sure that his hair didn't sparkle too. He and the Police Chief smiled at each other as if they shared a good joke. The Chief said to me 'This man speaks only Spanish. You will forgive my speaking it a moment?'

'Why not? You spoke it to me last night.' As he grew more suave I grew more brusque. I wondered how we should finish if we spent long together. While they talked I stood at an open window. It overlooked a courtyard where a fountain was playing. The soft lisping of the voices behind me mingled with the tinkle of the water in its white marble basin. Probably that fountain had been playing three or four hundred years, and there was something both sad and comforting in the thought that it would be playing all the mornings of my life while I sweated in noisy streets far away, never to see it again.

'He does not think your man is here, but we will look.' I turned from the window reluctantly and followed him upstairs. I've never seen a house less disorderly. Instead there was the earnest concentration of a chess tournament. We looked into room after room. Some were shuttered, some explosive with the collision of sunlight and white walls. Some were noisy, some so quiet I could hear the tinkling of my fountain. Sometimes the occupants were aware of us, sometimes not. Over them all the Chief waved a forgiving hand. 'So much flesh so early in the morning!' he murmured, shutting yet another door. Sometimes a woman spoke or beckoned us, and he laughed, but nothing else broke the monotony and I soon lost interest. I knew my man wasn't there. I'd told them in London he wouldn't be. He was somewhere in the green areas of the map, in the forests where an army could hide. 'You seem preoccupied,' said the Chief. 'It's not very interesting, I'm afraid.' He sounded like the apologetic proprietor of a third-rate circus. We left that house and visited others, identical except that none of them had a fountain. Coming out of the last I said, 'D'you ever wish you were back in the long grass again?' 'Senor,' he said. I looked round to see who Senor was. Apparently it was me, and the prelude to an unusually solemn pronouncement, for he stopped and faced me.

'Senor, there is a day for the long grass and a day to get out of it. Some of my friends lost count of the days. They lie out there for ever.' I knew then that he had changed sides. I knew then that he ought to have died with his friends, and that in some degree he had. But that was his problem. I had my own. We parted there. He put the car and driver at my disposal so I could look at the outlying country, and he walked back to headquarters.

The driver wasn't sounding our siren now. Perhaps it only went with the Chief. Perhaps, like me, he preferred quiet. The city is compact, and we were soon out of it on the mountain road. I've said there's a lot of forest. There's a lot of everything, forest and mountain and river and the plain – pampa, they call it – where the long grass grows. Everything except town. That's in a minority, and might vanish altogether, you feel, if the landscape pushed a bit harder. I could see the lot spread out below me like a map as we climbed. I didn't mind keeping my eyes open with this driver. He was a cautious lad, hugging the mountain and taking it slow. Somewhere down there my man was hiding. Maybe if I shouted he would put his head out. Like a line in a play I'd seen, something about 'Holler your name to the reverberating hills'. (Don't think I go to the theatre for pleasure. I was there on duty.) Up we went, into the sky. The driver stopped when we could go no higher and waved at the view as if I ought to get out and admire, so I did. It was worth looking at. It shimmered in the heat haze rising from it, and was silent with a silence so solid you could touch it. Far away I saw a line of white where the waters of the ocean broke on the shore. At that distance you got no sense of movement. And the man I wanted had all this. We drove on, dropping now toward the tree tops. Steam rose from them where the sun was evaporating the night dews, and the heat came up at you like hot hands. Now we could hear the shrieks of birds and the gibbering of animals. What had seemed perfect silence was in fact composed of a thousand noises, just as that apparently motionless whiteness on the shore was the effect of an endlessly repeated movement. Nothing was what it seemed, and that's an uncomfortable climate for my work. I fingered my revolver in its shoulder holster. We reckoned our man was armed and likely to resist arrest. So would I if I had a murder against me, a country for my playground and a million to spend on toys.

'Inca,' said the driver, pointing. It's the name of the

Indians who ruled there until the Spaniards thumped them in fifteen hundred and something. I looked round, expecting to see one, but there was nobody. 'Inca,' he repeated, still pointing, and then I saw ruins among the trees. I waved him on. I wasn't a tourist. We passed a luxury coach, full of people, going the opposite way. 'Inca,' he said again.

Later we arrived at a village. It confirmed the Police Chief's account of poverty. The people standing about had an appearance half Indian half Spanish. The two strains had not enhanced but rather neutralised each other. They'd forgotten how to be Indians without learning how to be Europeans, and stood in the sunlight with apathetic eyes. A few women were making basketwork or weaving cloth. I'd seen such things highly priced in London shops, and I wondered what fraction of that price was received here. There was no news of my man. The driver inquired, on his Chief's instructions, I suppose, and signified the empty result with gestures and head shaking. We drove out of the village, and some way beyond it I got my first view of the famous long grass. Acres of that feathery stuff you see in old ladies' gardens. But out there, growing densely, shoulder-high and rippling more like a sea that the real one, it's a different thing. I began to understand the Chief's obsession with it. I couldn't see its farther limits. Two or three horsemen moved in the middle distance. Only the horses' heads were visible. I should have liked to drive on, following my hunch, but my movements are watched more closely than the criminal's. I signalled the driver to turn back.

In the city the blue and green blinds of siesta were lowered. I found the Chief sitting on the raised terrace of a cafe. At the other tables men slept sternly, as if they had weighed the arguments for sleep and wake-fulness before deciding, but he stared straight in front of him. Perhaps he was afraid that if he shut his eyes death might catch him unawares.

'While you have been seeking clues,' he said, 'I have let them come to me.'

'Don't mystify me. I'm growing old.' I beckoned a waiter. At first I thought he disliked me personally, but watching him serve others I saw he simply disliked people.

'There is a ruined temple in the forest,' continued the Chief.

'I think I saw it.'

'There are several, but you may have seen this one. It is a tourist attraction. For years it had an unofficial custodian, an old half-breed with a smattering of lan-guages and a way with visitors. Today I hear he is dead.' So? Did he want a contribution to the wreath? 'Also I hear he has a successor. A white man.'

'That would be a crazy hiding-place.'

'If it seems so crazy that nobody looks, it would be a wise one.'

'Pull him in, then.'

'I may be wrong, and one mustn't advertise mistakes. Every afternoon in summer an excursion goes to the ruins. We have missed today's. I hoped you would be back sooner. But tomorrow we will join the excursion, mingle with the excursionists and take a look at the new custodian.' Having said this he began to drink in earnest, and I got no more sense out of him that after-noon. I suppose it was polite of him to have waited.

All that evening I wondered why he was being so helpful. I wondered alone, having turned down his invitation to join him. Let him topple over the cliff in his usual company. Being alone is my luxury, and it's perfect abroad. At home there's always somebody treading on the edges. After dinner I decided to reconnoitre the temple. A tourist isn't remarkable in ruins by moonlight. I slung a camera round my neck and said 'Inca' to a taxi driver. We were soon there, and, as I'd hoped, I wasn't the only visitor. It was an uncomfortable place. Terraces rising one above another. And pyramids. Not smooth sided like the Egyptian, but with steps cut in them, for the purpose of them had been at the top. They weren't built to a point, but stopped short in a small platform, and that had been the altar where human hearts were torn out for sacrifice. Anybody who took the job of caretaker here needed watching. I walked round, warily. The place oppressed me, as if it were balanced on my head. The moon was big. Shadows solid as masonry lay across my path. I kept well clear of those pyramids. A lump of stone let go from the top would have a respectable momentum by the time it reached bottom, which I'd rather not be there to measure. No sign of the new caretaker. Maybe like others of that profession he only took care not to be seen. Maybe he didn't live on the premises. I hadn't hoped to find him tonight. I wanted to familiarise myself with the lay-out of the place so I should know its short-cuts and emergency exits tomorrow. That done, I returned to my hotel and slept.

Next morning the Chief seemed no worse for his drinking, though it was hard for me to judge what might be better and worse with him. At least he was coherent. 'Today is the day!' he announced on seeing me.

'You're sure it's my man at the temple?'

'No, but anyway it will be amusing.'

I remembered he'd said the same about our tour of the Houses, so I didn't fix my hopes too high. 'It's kind of you to take a hand yourself,' I said. 'Specially after saying you wouldn't.'

'At this time of year I find the streets constricting. I shall enjoy an escape.'

'Shan't we be a bit too near the long grass for you?'

He smiled, like an adult smiling at a child's view of something. Perhaps for him the long grass wasn't a place any more, but a state of mind.

'I saw the beginning of it yesterday,' I persisted, trying to force his explanation. 'It looked like a sea. There were three horsemen. You felt they would sink deeper and deeper until they drowned.'

'You should be careful,' he said.

We played cards until excursion time. Business seemed slack. Or perhaps they didn't bother him with routine. We didn't talk any more. Only the click of cards on the desk. Just before two we settled our debts and walked to the excursion depot, accompanied at a distance by several of his men. The other passengers were holidaymakers who didn't look at us twice, but I noticed a stiffening in the driver's attitude, and his observance of speed limits was exemplary. The Chief sat beside me, staring at something out of sight as usual. I heard without listening the guide's commentary on what we passed and on the treat ahead. At the temple we were free to follow the guide or please ourselves. The other police went with the crowd, but the Chief held me back a moment. 'I should like you to have my gun,' he said.

'There's nothing wrong with mine.'

'To please me.'

I accepted. I didn't intend using a gun if I could help it.

'And may I have yours?' he said.

An old South American custom? I examined the

revolver he'd lent me. I hadn't lost by the swop. We hurried to catch up with the crowd, not wanting to attract attention. The temple looked different in sunlight, like a room where you've had bad dreams. But you know the dreams are only hiding. They might be hiding in my companion's head. I mean a remembrance of blood-thirsty gods must linger, a remembrance of ancestors ready to spill and shed blood for them.

'D'you think he's had a tip-off?' I asked.

'I am confident he hasn't.'

Everybody else's confidence worried me. In London they were confident he would hide in a town, simply because they'd pledged themselves to catch him quick and there was only a handful of towns against a lifetime of wilderness. I was the only one who wasn't confident, and on top of making me feel unsociable that meant I should get the blame when everybody else's confidence proved wrong. Still we mooched round with the tourists. Still no sign of our suspect. The weaker of the party began to straggle, and the Chief took the chance to send out scouts. When they reported he said, 'The man is here but keeping out of sight. We must wait until the coach leaves.'

When the coach had gone the ruins were strangely silent. Shadows of late afternoon lay on them, and soon the bad dreams would emerge. I was conscious of being among natives, who might respond unpleasantly to the influence of the place. I wanted my man alive.

'Let's start before it's dark,' I said. 'Where is he?'

'We will drive him this way so you can make the arrest.'

'Does everybody understand there's to be no shooting if it can possibly be avoided?'

'Of course.'

I was left alone in what I suppose had been a street.

It felt more like an arena now. I waited, watching sunset colour the stone. If they didn't hurry we should lose him in the dark. Even now recognition would be impossible until I was near enough to make an easy target. The low sun would be behind him, too. I waited. They were taking their time. The air had cooled and the colour was nearly gone when two shots splintered the silence.

'He's coming your way,' shouted the Chief. 'And he's shooting.'

A figure appeared on the top terrace, silhouetted against the last of the light. I saw the gun in his hand and saw him raise it.

'You'll only make it worse for yourself,' I called, dropping flat. He stood a moment. The light was too poor for me to risk a shot. Then he retreated over the skyline. I ran up the terraces. When I reached the top the sun's last glimmer had sunk right down to the horizon and my man had vanished. After a while I found the Chief.

'He came back your way,' I said. 'How did he get past you?'

'We drove him your way. Why didn't you shoot?'

'The light was too bad. I couldn't be sure of only laming him.'

'I fired, but he was zig-zagging up the terraces.'

'Between us we made a pretty poor show,' I muttered angrily. He was angry, too. Angrier, maybe. He recalled his men. I hoped to see a prisoner among them, but they brought only their sullen selves and stood staring at us as if wondering what the excitement was about. A search of the ruins found nothing. 'At least we're on the right track,' said the Chief. 'A man with a gun who shoots when challenged is likely to be the man you want.'

'Did he answer?'

'No. But I spoke English and obviously he understood.'

'Did you recognise him from his photograph?'

'The light was poor. So was the photograph.'

'He can't have gone far. Let's get after him.'

'He can't have gone far, but nor can we without transport or lights. I will call up more men and at dawn we will search again. He can't go far before then and he shall not escape a second time. But next time you must not be afraid of shooting.'

I bit back a retort.

We spent the night in that village I'd seen the day before. Its apathetic people received us without surprise or welcome. The Chief and I shared a hut which its owners vacated for us after giving us food. Having eaten, I wrapped myself in a blanket. There was nothing else to do. I slept badly. Something in our evening's misadventure troubled me. I couldn't see it clear. I couldn't see how my man had escaped unless the Chief had let him, nor why the Chief was so angry with me. Maybe he was a coward. Maybe he'd funked the arrest. Maybe he was angry with himself, and was simply passing it on to me. But he seemed too smooth a character for that. Waking and dozing I puzzled over it. Every time I woke I saw him smoking at the window. At dawn he shook me. They'd brought us cups of a foul brew they called coffee, and horses were ready outside. I'd never ridden before, bar falling off a cart horse when I was three, and these were bareback, so you can imagine the picture I made. But even that didn't raise a smile among the villagers. We set off, the Chief riding beside me and keeping a hand on my reins. He had mustered many more men for today's hunt and we made a formidable posse. Still I wondered

why, after his first show of indifference, he was taking
so active a part in my business, and how he'd over-
come his dread of the long grass – for that was obviously where we were heading. Perhaps he'd had
orders.

We took the same road I'd been driven along yesterday. There was the pampa rippling in front of us.
The sun was still low, and hit you full in the eyes
across the top of it. We plunged in, the horses immediately up to their necks like those I'd seen. The
men unslung the rifles from their shoulders. I glanced
at my companion's face. There was no sign of emotion,
but his habitual dark glasses and a borrowed sombrero
didn't leave much room. Borrowing hats had been a
good idea. Already the sun was fierce. When it got on
top of us it would hammer any uncovered man into
the ground and leave him there. Until reaching the
pampa we'd ridden in a group, but entering it the men
spread out, on instinct or command, into a single rank
of which the Chief and I were the centre. And so we
advanced, the intervals between riders increasing until
the line was as extended as it could be without any man
losing sight of his immediate neighbours. Behind this
line walked several villagers holding dogs on long
leashes. These brutes showed none of their masters'
apathy. Only the Chief and I rode together. I couldn't
see either end of our line. Nor could I see any limit to
the plain on either side, but I guessed those limits lay
even farther than the farthest riders. All I could see
was the man on left of me, the Chief, the man on his
right and the grass going on for ever. All I could hear
was the grass giving way to the horses' legs as they
advanced at a steady pace and the panting of the dogs.
Nobody spoke. The Chief sat his horse badly, slouched,
yet he scarcely needed the reins to govern it, often

letting them go and using only his legs. As ever, his eyes were fixed on something out of sight. The men riding beside us scanned the ground with a regular glance from side to side, like the sweep of a scythe. The whole operation reminded me of harvesting. I pictured the fugitive running before us, silly with terror, to seek the diminishing cover that remained, as I'd seen small animals run. Supposing he was in the pampa, as the Chief believed. I couldn't make out his reasons for believing it. The trouble with a foreigner speaking English is that you can never be sure he means what he says. Like a parrot. The sun was rising fast and its heat was a fist in your face.

'What's beyond this plain?' I asked.

'The river.'

'Can he cross it? Going so slowly we may not catch him this side.'

'He'll never reach it. A horse can walk comfortably through the grass. Not so a man, who must force not only his legs but his whole body through. He'll be exhausted long before the river.'

I felt almost sorry for him. Was what he'd done worth all this? His crime wasn't clear to me. I knew there was a precise killing and an approximate million in it, but whether he'd done the murder to get the money or to keep it or to conceal it I never knew. I even tried not to think of him by name. That only makes it worse, as giving a name to your chickens makes it harder to wring their necks.

At midday we dismounted to rest. The horses lay down to escape the sun and we followed their example. The villagers had brought provisions for us. I ate some kind of fruit mess, which tasted better than it looked, and drank water. Lying in the grass I felt like a kid again. It reminded me of lying on my face in a meadow pretending the grass was a jungle. I could see none of our party except the Chief. He wasn't talking. He wasn't drinking, either, though he carried a flask of wine. I lay with my hat pulled over my eyes, inhaling the smell of horses and grass, wondering about the man in front. Our disappearance must have seemed a miracle to him. But he would know better. No lunch break for him, poor devil. I fell asleep then. I was woken by the Chief's shaking me, and couldn't remember at first where I was or what I had to get up for.

Consequently we were later mounting than the rest and moved off a bit behind them. The Chief did nothing to mend this gap, so we were thrown into a kind of isolation, if not intimacy, where I felt bound to break silence.

'Does this remind you of the old days?' I asked.

Slowly he turned his head, as if it had a long way to go, and long he stared at me, as if he'd never seen me before. Then he said, 'Where is yesterday?' I didn't know where it was. I was making conversation, not opening a metaphysical conference. 'It is here,' he continued, tapping his forehead. 'Not there,' sweeping a dismissive hand across the landscape. 'And where is tomorrow?' I kept my mouth tight shut. 'Here too,' tapping again. 'And where are yesterday and tomorrow when the brain stops?' I was sorry I'd mentioned it.

The regular movement of the horses and the monotony of the scene were hypnotic. A lot of time slipped by without my noticing, until I saw the sky getting that old familiar flush. This would be the fourth sunset I'd seen in that country and I didn't want to see many more.

'His stamina's better than you expected,' I said. 'It'll be dark soon.'

'We shall catch him this side of the river,' he repeated. 'I have an instinct for these things.'

'How far's the river?'

'We shall catch him before dark. That is when a fugitive loses hope.'

'I should have thought it was when he gained it.'

'It's not pursuit that exhausts a man. It's anxiety. Pursuit stops and starts, but anxiety is incessant. Sooner or later comes a night when you can't bear the prospect of the sun rising again on uncertainty. So you stand and wait for them.'

Was that how it had been with him? During my trance we'd lagged farther behind the line and even the villagers with their dogs had got in front of us. It seemed a daft position for the commander – his men beyond call and his rear unguarded. I kept looking over my shoulder. If my man had somehow slipped through the line, we two stragglers might present an irresistible target. Specially if he had a silencer. These backward glances strengthened my fancy that the pampa was a sea. Now we were far out on it. I could see no perimeter, no firm ground. In the nearly invisible distance was what might be a mountain range but might equally be a bank of clouds. My companion said a river lay not far in front, but for all evidence of it the grass might go on for ever, to the edge of the world.

He stopped and put a hand on my arm. The air had begun to turn opaque and I shivered at its sudden chill. 'He is near,' he whispered. 'I sense it.'

'How did he give them the slip?' I asked, nodding at the distant sombreros.

'They are townsmen,' he replied scornfully.

'Let's fire a shot to turn them back.'

'No. This one is artful. We must not alarm him. Dismount – but quietly.' I slipped off to stand beside him.

'Stay here with the horses,' he said, 'and I will find him.'

'He's my man.'

'But this is not your country. You have my gun still? Then don't be afraid to use it.'

'Don't be eager to use mine,' I said, detaining him.

'I shall do only what is necessary.' He looked at me a moment, then evaporated into the grass. That's how I can best describe the swiftness and silence of his action. A flash of old fieldcraft, justifying his contempt for townsmen. I stood between the horses for cover and kept a watch all round. The radius of vision was short now. No sound but the fidgeting of the horses. If the Chief was moving, it was with the same deadly soundlessness I'd admired. The other man must have equal cunning, though recalling his dossier I couldn't imagine where he'd learnt it. I couldn't tell where either of them was. One each side of me perhaps. I hoped they wouldn't hit the referee.

'He's coming towards you,' called the Chief. 'Be careful.' The advice seemed superfluous. I drew my gun, pushed off the safety catch and slowly turned. I had a good few hundredweight of horsemeat to shield me, but bits remained exposed. Like my head. Then I saw a movement – a slight movement of the grass just as I was turning away from it in my slow spin. It was checked immediately. I called him by name then. 'Give up,' I said. 'There's a troop of trigger-happy cowboys in front. We're both off our home ground here. Come out with your hands high and we can be on a plane for England tonight.'

He fired. It annoyed me that he should be vicious enough to shoot and silly enough to miss.

'Do that again and I'll fire,' I said.

He did it again, hitting my shoulder, and I kept my

promise. He fell forward out of the grass. It was the Chief, and he was dead.

I knew the answer to the riddle. I opened his gun – my gun – to confirm it. Only two shots left. Two fired at the temple last night, two fired now. The man I was looking for had fired none, because he'd never been there to fire any. Only the Chief, tired of running away from death. The comrades he'd betrayed were dead or in prison, but they must have relatives. Endless ramifications of revenge. Tired of looking over his shoulder, he had appointed me his executioner.

The shooting had attracted his men, who returned through the dusk like a slow cortege.

Why hadn't he done it himself? Later I heard rumours of a wife behind shutters somewhere. The pension, maybe? Perhaps there was a suicide clause. Perhaps giving me his gun had been the nearest he could get.

The man I wanted was caught in Birmingham.

OPERATION CASH

by Michael Underwood

The intercom on Terry Mears' desk gave a brisk, demanding buzz as though an indignant insect was trapped inside. Terry leaned forward and depressed a switch to hear the voice of one of the firm's senior partners.

'Mears?'

'Yes, Mr Bisgood.'

'I've got Mrs Tonbridge on the outside line. She doesn't remember having had a stock transfer form for the Consolidated Stores we sold for her last week. Can you check whether it was sent to her? It certainly should have been,' he added accusingly.

'It was. And she's returned it signed.'

'You're quite sure about that?'

'Absolutely certain, Mr Bisgood. If you wish, I'll ...'

'No, that's good enough.'

There was a click, followed by silence, leaving Terry staring at the intercom with resentment. Resentment directed not at the apparatus itself, nor even at Mr Bisgood though he qualified for some, but at Mrs Tonbridge and a host of other clients of the firm.

For a not very highly paid clerk, there was something distinctly unsettling in spending your working days handling bits of paper relating to other people's money. Money meaning, for the most part, gains and profits in stock market deals.

Take Mrs Tonbridge for example. She had made a clear three thousand pounds profit on the sale of her Consolidated Stores shares. Mr Bisgood had advised her to buy them. Mr Bisgood had advised her to sell them. She just sat back in her Knightsbridge flat and collected, unable even to remember signing a transfer form a few days previously. She didn't deserve to have all that money. It wasn't fair.

Terry got up and walked across to a grimy window and stared out. The view was of another building with rows of grimy windows. At one of them a young man about his own age was also gazing out. Terry wondered whether he ever had similar thoughts to his own. . . .

Like tens of thousands of other young men working in London, Terry inhabited bed-sitterland. His particular pad was not far from King's Cross Station. During the five years he had been working for his firm in the City, he had moved a dozen times, but had finally reached the dismal conclusion that on his money he was never going to get anything better in the way of a lodging.

Admittedly, his salary had almost doubled in the course of five years, but £1650 p.a. still fell short by a few thousands of what he thought he should have. Small wonder he was galled by his position. All around him money flowed, but none of it into his pocket.

During the past year he had spent an increasing number of his spare moments contemplating ways of getting rich – quickly. But they all required capital in the first instance. And Terry Mears not only didn't possess capital, but could see no way of laying his hands on any. Not legitimately, that is.

And so his mind had turned to various illegitimate ways of acquiring money. At first, he had been quite carried away by the number of exciting prospects which seemed suddenly to be within his reach.

His own job, as clerk in charge of all stock transfers,

was positively rich in opportunities for well-concealed fraud. Well concealed? There lay the snag. Later, if not sooner, the most ingenious scheme was certain to become uncovered and then its perpetrator swapped his city suit for prison garb and disappeared from view for a period.

Terry could see no fun in that. But the more he thought about it, the more determined he became to work out a foolproof scheme for making money. It must be possible. As he walked along the streets by day and lay in bed in his shabby room by night, he forced his mind into thinking of nothing else. But for a long time it seemed hopeless, every scheme had its flaw. And flaws spelt prison.

And then one day not long after Mrs Tonbridge had sold her Consolidated Stores shares, something happened to send his hopes soaring. Not that he immediately recognised the sudden possibilities of quick, easy money that had been presented to him. But the seed was sown and it didn't take long to burst into wild growth. What happened was this.

It was his custom to cash a weekly cheque each Thursday lunchtime at the Moorgate branch of the City and Provincial Bank which carried his account. On this particular Thursday, Mr Bisgood had sent him up to the West End with a sheaf of share transfer forms for signature by the Company Secretary of one of the firm's corporation clients. He was to wait until they were signed and bring them back to the office. He arrived, however, to find that the Company Secretary had temporarily disappeared and by the time he had hung about and then got caught in a traffic jam, he arrived back in the city only shortly before his bank closed. He was telling all this to the rather attractive girl teller who was cashing his cheque when she said :

'Haven't you got one of our cheque cards?'

'No. I hadn't really thought about it,' he answered.

'You should ask for one. I think you'd find it useful. It'll enable you to cash a cheque up to £30 at any branch of any bank.'

'Any bank?'

'Yes, any.' She smiled as though happy to be able to bestow such splendid tidings. 'Every bank will honour a City and Provincial card. And you can't walk far in any direction without coming across a bank, can you?'

'That's true,' he said thoughtfully. 'Can I apply for one now?'

'Certainly.' A few seconds later, Terry had completed the necessary form. 'You should receive your card within a few days,' the girl said. 'I'm sure you'll find it saves you a lot of bother.'

Terry thanked her and walked back to his office.

Three days later, the cheque card arrived by recorded delivery. Enclosed was a leaflet explaining the benefits of having become its owner. The bank made it sound as if Terry had come through some arcane test of responsible citizenship with flying colours and the card was his coveted prize.

He signed his name with a ballpoint pen on the white strip which ran across the centre of the plastic card and slipped it into his wallet.

The following week he used it to cash a modest cheque at a branch of another bank. He was surprised how simple it was. Within a day or so, the seed which had been craftily sown by its acquisition began to grow.

The climactic moment came as he was standing on a traffic island in the city waiting for the lights to change. He glanced casually around him and became suddenly aware that he had three different banks within his line of vision. He turned his head. There were two more. He looked in the other direction. One more. Six banks within eighty yards of where he was standing. That represented £180. His gaze roamed around the six facades again. £180 within easy reach. Allow five minutes per bank including the short walk to the next and it worked out at £180 in something like half an hour.

That evening when he got home, he sat down with pencil and paper and did some sums. He reckoned there probably weren't many areas where you'd find six banks within such a confined space. Even so it should be possible to find districts where several were grouped conveniently together. Supposing you allowed for visiting eight banks an hour, that would represent £240. And as banks were open for business five hours a day, that would mean a haul of £1200.

He stared at the figure mesmerised. Then underneath it, he wrote 'say £1000' and drew a circle round it. After all, one had to allow for mishaps; moreover, he wasn't going to find forty banks (his day's optimum total) all within walking distance of one another.

He put the piece of paper and pencil on the bed beside him and gazed at the dirt-engrained wall in front of him. But his mind was too busy to notice either the dirty marks or even the wall itself.

At the end, he had worked out a rough plan of campaign.

The first thing was to open an account in a false name at another branch of the City and Provincial. Not a branch in London as he knew that cheques cashed within the London area took less time to clear if the account was also held in London. And as London was the obvious place for his intended operations, the account should be at a branch in the provinces. Not too small a branch and at the same time not a headquarters one. He would select a medium sized branch in a suburban area of one of the northern industrial towns. Somewhere like Blackburn or Huddersfield. Cheques cashed in London on a branch up there would, he reckoned, take three days to clear.

That would give him three days to operate. Namely Wednesday, Thursday and Friday. Three hectic days at the end of which he should be about £3000 richer. £3000 in three days. Almost twice what he earned in three hundred and sixty-five days. By Monday, of course, the game would be over. The returned cheques would be pouring back to the branch which held the account and the alarm bells would be sounding in the offices of a large number of bank managers, though none louder than in that of the manager of the branch he finally selected for this rare old pounding.

He would open an account at this branch a nice distance from London and keep it fairly active so as not to arouse suspicion. And when they had become used to having his account he would apply for a cheque card.

A sudden thought came to him and he seized the pencil and piece of paper again. £3000 in three days was going to involve an awful lot of cheques. One hundred to be precise. Well, there was no reason why the bank should refuse him a book containing that number. He'd better have a second book of, say, fifty in case the scheme exceeded his wildest hopes and he could step up his productivity. But these were details which he could attend to nearer the time. At the moment he was concerned only with the broad plan.

As to the cashing of the cheques, that was going to require much more planning. Moreover, luck was going to be an element over which no amount of planning could have any control. For example, he knew from experience of cashing cheques at his own bank that sometimes the place was virtually empty and at exactly the same hour of the same day of the following week there'd be a queue at each teller's position. Weather would also play a part as people took twice as long to cash cheques when it was wet what with all the fumbling and undoing of sodden garments. As weather could clearly be an important factor, perhaps he ought to study the long-range forecast before finally picking his D-day.

He would spend the coming week-end in an intensive reconnaissance.

When he set out on Saturday morning to visit the prospective scenes of his forthcoming depredations, he had done a further amount of ground-work. Having provisionally decided on the districts in which he was going to operate, he had consulted telephone directories and reference books in the office to ensure that all the banks were well represented in these areas. Not that he anticipated any problems on this aspect for he had become particularly bank conscious since his scheme had begun to fertilise and had been surprised to discover what a prolific species they were. Where there was a branch of one, you'd almost certainly find most of the others established within stone-throwing distance.

In the result he decided to concentrate on the western suburbs one day, those in the south-east of London on the next and the northern suburbs on the last day of operations.

It was a gloriously sunny day as he left his lodgings and walked briskly to King's Cross Underground Station. The month was June and he felt the weather was an omen for the success of his scheme, even though it was still a long way off fulfilment. But this was the first piece of physical activity towards its accomplishment. His plan had, so to speak, left the drawing-board stage, though there would doubtless be further paperwork to be undertaken.

His idea was to start in Acton, move on to Ealing and then proceed westwards through the succession of suburbs which straddled the Uxbridge Road. If time permitted he would recce the northern scene of operations in the afternoon and reserve Sunday for his survey in the south-east. In the event, however, he had only completed his recce of one area by late afternoon, by which time he was both tired and ready to return home to sort out his information.

The first thing he had realised was that he was going to need a car in order to move quickly from one cluster of banks to the next. To depend on public transport was to squander precious time. There was also the point that by the end of each day of operation he was going to be fairly encumbered with cash and he certainly didn't want to be lugging a heavy bag of £5 notes on and off public transport. However, a car presented no problem. He'd hire one for the three days. A mini van would be best.

With a car and with the groupings of banks he had now seen, he reckoned he should be able to average between six and eight banks per hour. In two of the areas he had surveyed, he considered he could comfortably visit six banks in half an hour, so conveniently were they situated to each other. But traffic being what it was in those congested parts, he was bound to lose time in moving on to the next group.

He was blessed with a good memory for detail and also with an above average bump of locality so that he made the minimum number of notes of his day's activity. All he recorded was the number of banks in each of the areas visited and the best place for parking a car while he made his calls.

The next day, Sunday, encouraged by the success of Saturday's recce and by the still glorious weather, he set out and covered his chosen area in the north of London. Give or take a bank or two, the result was the same as the previous day's. As, indeed, was the outcome of his final recce the following Saturday when he travelled down to Lewisham as the centre of his prospective operations in that area. Again the weather could be seen only as a splendid omen.

By this time he had provisionally fixed the second week in August for executing his scheme. He was due for some holiday in that month and he also reckoned that with so many people being away from London in August, the banks were likely to be less crowded. But then, of course, there'd probably be fewer staff on duty as presumably bank clerks also took holidays in August. He shrugged. There were no mathematical certainties, all he could do was to plan in as much detail as he could, foresee as many snags as possible and then hope for the best.

On the Saturday following his two week-ends of reconnoitring at the London end of operations, he travelled up to Lancashire.

He arrived in Manchester before lunch and in the early afternoon took a bus to Blackburn, having selected this town as the one in which to open what he thought of as his widow's cruse. Twenty-four miles from Manchester and a population of around a hundred thousand seemed to invest it with the desired degree of off-centre anonymity. While the bus was still passing through the outskirts he spotted a branch of the City and Provincial Bank and got off at the next stop.

It looked just what he wanted, a medium-sized branch on the outskirts of a medium-sized town well away from anywhere he was proposing to be seen.

He noted down the bank's address, crossed the street and caught the next bus back to Manchester. A couple of hours later he was on an express train to London.

In retrospect he wondered whether it hadn't been an unnecessary journey, but there was something satis-factory in having seen with his own eyes the branch at which he was intending to open the account.

The next day, using an accommodation address in Bayswater, he wrote to the bank (with a ballpoint pen and in a heavily disguised hand), saying that he would shortly be moving to Blackburn from London and would like to open an account and would they please send him the necessary particulars. He added that he hadn't hitherto held a bank account and he wondered whether it would be all right to pay £200 in for a start. (This sum represented the greater part of his savings and he pictured the knowing look of amusement on the manager's face as he read this naive touch.) He signed the letter 'F. Barr' and then printed beneath the signature 'FRANCIS BARR'.

He had given a fair amount of thought to his new name. It had to be short and the sort that could be signed in a scrawl. And Francis somehow endowed it with an air of respectability, though he would only sign as F. Barr.

He had also taken care to find the sort of accom-modation address at which no questions were asked of its clients, even though you had to pay a bit extra for this admirable discretion. Five days later, he called there and picked up a letter bearing the Blackburn postmark. He waited until he got home before opening the envelope. Inside was a courteous reply from the manager saying how delighted he was that Mr Barr wished to open an account at his branch and that a deposit of £200 would be entirely satisfactory. If Mr Barr would just fill in the enclosed forms, the necessary formalities could soon be completed.

One of the forms asked for two specimen signatures, another invited him to apply for a cheque-book and a third called for the names of two references. He had anticipated this last requirement and planned accordingly.

For an additional fee, with no questions asked, the man who ran the accommodation address had put him in touch with someone who had a small business off Praed Street. What the business was he never asked or found out, other than that the supply of false references was part of it. It was run from a drab room above a porno shop by a man with shifty eyes and a rancid odour. He had demanded £15 on account and a further £15 when the references had been satisfactorily supplied.

A week later, he collected a further letter from the bank which informed him of their 'very real pleasure' in opening an account for Mr F. Barr and of their hope of being able to be of the utmost service to him. He smiled, for that was just what he intended they should be.

He sent off £200 by registered post in ten £20 notes and in the ensuing month drew a number of small cheques on the account and also paid in a further £35.

At the end of that period, he wrote a letter to the manager saying that his transfer north had been held up and that, in these circumstances, it would be a great convenience if he could have one of their cheque cards to enable him to cash cheques elsewhere. Also a new cheque-book containing a hundred cheques.

Both were duly despatched to him without demur.

It was time to hire the mini van.

The planning stage was finally over and he was all set to go.

Even the weather forecast was on his side.

A cardiograph would probably have registered a few extra heart beats as Terry Mears entered the first of the banks that Wednesday morning in the second week of August, but to all outward appearances, he was his usual cool, detached self.

He had encountered no difficulty in parking the van and here he was at three minutes past ten (he had felt it better not to be actually on the doorstep when the doors were unlocked) entering the Acton branch of the City and Provincial. There were three tellers' positions, though only two tellers were on duty. One, a girl, was already dealing with a customer; the other, a young man, was having a prodigious yawn. Terry went straight over and passed across the cheque for £30, which he had already made out, together with F. Barr's cheque card. The teller glanced at the signature on the cheque and then at that on the card.

'How do you want it?' he asked in a bored tone as he returned the card and began another yawn.

'Fives, please.'

The teller counted out six, re-counted them and pushed them in Terry's direction.

The whole operation had lasted under two minutes and the young man had scarcely accorded him a glance. Exhilarated, he walked briskly to the next bank which was only fifty yards away. Again everything went as smoothly as he could have hoped. It was the same at the third and the fourth. £120 in under half an hour! He could scarcely believe how easy it was. Euphoric as he felt, be realised, however, that he was bound to encounter some snags before the day was out and, indeed, did so at the next bank he entered.

There was only one teller on duty, a grey-haired woman who was already attending to one customer while another waited. Terry joined the short queue and watched impatiently as she laboriously counted out ten £1 notes, checked them and re-checked them. What the hell was a stupid old cow like her doing in a bank!

At last the customer got his money and moved away. The man behind him took his place and to Terry's utter dismay produced a paying-in book and a bundle of cheques which he handed to the old cow. Christ, he'd be here the rest of the day! He looked round desperately to see whether one of the clerks at the back of the bank mightn't take pity on him and come forward. He quickly told himself, however, to remain calm. He mustn't do anything to draw attention to himself, anything which might cause anyone to remember him subsequently.

At last his turn came and he passed across his cheque and the bank card.

'You've already signed it,' the grey-haired woman said. 'You shouldn't have done. Kindly sign it again on the back.'

Terry almost felt the policeman's hand on his sleeve as she handed the cheque back to him and got ready to watch him sign while she held his cheque card in her hand.

Thank God he'd signed 'F. Barr' enough times to be able to do so even under cold scrutiny. He fingered the cheque back to her and watched her compare this further signature with that on the card.

'How do you want it?' she asked.

'Fives, please.'

Slowly she counted them out as though they were from her personal stock and did a second and then a third count before handing him the money. Terry picked them up and forced himself to walk unhurriedly out of the bank. He felt he'd been in there several hours, but in fact it was only twelve minutes. Even so he couldn't afford (and 'afford' was the right word, he reflected grimly) to have that experience too often.

And, happily, he didn't. He lost a bit of time around lunchtime when the banks tended to be more full, but by the end of the day he had cashed cheques to the tune of £930. It niggled him that he hadn't reached his four figure target. Nevertheless it was a fair day's haul and he might be able to improve on it the next day.

And so it turned out to be, Thursday bringing him £1020. He returned home that evening weary but triumphant, after parking the van as usual in the multi-storey garage about half a mile from his lodging.

£1950 in two days! It was fantastic! But he felt he'd almost used up all his nervous resources. He felt absolutely whacked, both physically and mentally. But it was the exhaustion of the Olympic gold medallist. An exhaustion born of triumph.

When he set out the next morning, it was with a feeling of confidence mixed with relief. He realised that there was a possibility that some of the cheques he had cashed on Wednesday might be arriving at F. Barr's bank in Blackburn. It seemed likely that some might be cleared quicker than others, but even if this was so, he knew that no general alert could be put out before Monday. Thus even though there was a greater risk today than on the two previous days, it was still a very minor one. Indeed, he had quite forgotten its existence by the time he had visited his first six banks (it was his day for south-east London) without a hitch arising.

And then something happened which no amount of forethought could have foreseen, no amount of planning could have prevented. At the time it seemed like sheer, outrageous bad luck. . . .

It was a couple of minutes after eleven o'clock and he had just entered the Lewisham branch of the City and Provincial. It looked almost deserted. There wasn't a customer in sight and apart from the sole teller on duty, a pale-faced, long-haired young man with a fashionably drooping moustache, the only sign of life were the voices of two girls whose heads were silhouetted against a glass panel behind the teller's position.

He approached the teller and passed over his cheque card and the already made-out cheque. Since that first morning, he had only twice been asked to re-sign a cheque in the teller's presence and accordingly he had not altered his practice of presenting them fully made-out, including signature. Whatever the rules, it was clear that most bank clerks were satisfied with comparing the signature already on the cheque with that on the card.

Something about the teller's manner caught his notice. He appeared nervous, with his mind on other things. Twice he glanced at his watch in the course of counting out six £5 notes and he seemed deliberately to avoid looking in Terry's direction. But why should Terry care!

He had picked up his money and just turned away

when he became aware that someone had entered the bank through the further door. What made him turn to look at the newcomer, he never knew. But some prickling of his senses made him look round.

A slim, heavily bearded young man was at the counter. Even as Terry glanced at him, a gun materialised in one hand while the other reached forward and seized a swollen bag from the teller's side of the counter. The next moment there was a loud explosion as the gun went off and Terry took to his heels.

He had parked the van at a meter about a hundred yards away and he made his way there as fast as he decently could without drawing attention to himself. Even as he drew away from the kerb, the raucous sounds of converging police cars filled the air.

It was out of the question visiting other banks in the immediate area and as this had been the first of six, it meant abandoning £150. His next cluster was over two miles away and though he drove in the direction, he wasn't sure whether he was ready to go on. For a time, he couldn't think straight. He felt himself in a state of shock and his mind was all confused.

Eventually he turned up a quiet side road and parked. He lit a cigarette to try and calm himself. After a while he was able to sort his thoughts into some order. The first thing his mind registered was that he had clearly been the only witness of what had happened. But had anyone observed his own departure from the bank? If not, the only person who could definitely speak of his presence was the bearded robber, as even the teller, out of whose line of vision he had moved, probably wouldn't have known whether he was still in the bank or not. Unhappily, however, it was beyond dispute that F. Barr had cashed a cheque there only seconds before the robbery took place.

Calmer, but still shaken by his experience, he decided to abandon the rest of the day's operation. It meant writing off about £800, but he didn't trust himself not to make some silly giveaway slip. His nerve had cracked and it was better to acknowledge the fact and play safe.

He turned in the van on his way home and by one o'clock was back in his lodging. He spent the next hour destroying every reminder of F. Barr's existence. The cheque card, the unused cheques and everything that connected him with the Blackburn branch of the City and Provincial Bank.

And all the time something nagged at the back of his mind. There had been something about the robbery which puzzled him, but which maddeningly eluded him.

About five o'clock he went out and bought the evening papers. His eye was immediately arrested by a headline on an inner page of the *Standard* which read: BANK SHOOTING DRAMA. Beneath this came: 'A bearded young man entered the Lewisham branch of the City and Provincial Bank this morning, held the teller up at gunpoint and made off with a haul of £10,000. All in a matter of seconds, but not before he had fired a shot over the teller's head when the latter made to stall him off. 25-year-old Mr Rodney Purling told the police how he found himself suddenly looking down the barrel of a gun while the bearded gunman quietly demanded the bag of fivers which was awaiting collection by Brightson's the well-known South East London store. "I tried to distract him while I reached for the alarm and it was then that he fired. I realised he really meant business and I pushed the bag towards him. It was all over in a matter of seconds. The bank was empty at the time as far as I know." The only casualty was a clock on the back wall of the bank which was shattered by the bullet.'

The other paper carried a similar account of what had happened and included a photograph of Rodney Purling with 'his attractive twenty-two-year-old blonde actress fiancee, Candy Bishop'. Mr Purling and Miss Bishop, it told its readers, were hoping to get married at Christmas. Miss Bishop's home was in Northampton and Mr Purling lived at 19 Laker Road, Greenwich.

Terry read both accounts a second time and then sat back in deep thought.

At the end of five minutes, a knowing smile crept across his face and he nodded his head slowly in a satisfied way. The more he thought about it, the surer he became. Perhaps the day need not turn out to be such a dead loss after all. . . .

At six o'clock the next evening, he rang the bell of 19 Laker Road. The door was opened by Rodney Purling himself. He looked anxious and furtive.

'If you're from the press . . .' he began.

Terry smiled. 'No, I'm nothing to do with the press. I'd just like to have a chat with you.'

'Who are you?'

'You obviously don't recognise me then?'

Purling frowned. 'Should I?'

'No, I'm not really surprised you don't remember me.' Terry's tone was amused. 'The only time we met, you obviously had much more important things on your mind. You were expecting someone else any moment.'

Purling's frown increased. 'I'm sorry, but I'm not following you. And I'm afraid I'm rather busy. . . .'

'Yes,' Terry went on comfortably, 'you were expecting a robbery to take place.'

Purling's jaw fell and his expression was one of such comical amazement that Terry laughed outright.

'Now may I come in?' he asked, at the same time walking past Purling into the hall.

Purling closed the front door.

'Who are you?' he asked in a frightened voice.

'Which room can we talk in?' Terry looked about him.

'Upstairs.'

'You lead the way.'

As they entered a room which looked out on the garden at the back, a girl stared at them from the only armchair.

'Miss Bishop, isn't it? I recognise you from your photograph in last night's evening paper.'

Candy Bishop made no answer, but looked at her fiance with an expression of nervous inquiry.

'I think you'd better say who you are and what you're doing here,' Purling said stonily.

'My name is Barr. Does that jog your memory? ... No, apparently not. ... Well, I happened to be cashing a cheque just before you were robbed yesterday. But, as I say, I'm not surprised you don't remember me as you obviously had much weightier things on your mind at the time.' He paused, but neither the young man nor the girl spoke. They just stared at him as though mesmerised. Terry looked at them for a second, then his expression which had been one of self-indulgent amusement became suddenly sterner. 'The thing is I know the robbery was a put-up job and I want a share of the proceeds or I'll go to the police. Your choice is a bit less money and freedom or the certainty of jail.'

'He's bluffing,' the girl said.

'Want to test me?'

'You've no evidence of anything,' Purling said defiantly. 'You'd better go before I throw you out.'

'Yes, before we send for the police,' the girl chimed in.

Terry felt in his pocket and pulled out a small plastic envelope.

'I'm sure you have a great future ahead of you as an actress, Miss Bishop. Particularly playing bearded male parts. But you must be careful not to shed your own pretty blonde hairs about the stage.' He held up the envelope. 'One long blonde hair recovered from the floor of the City and Provincial Bank at approximately five minutes past eleven yesterday morning. I think the police would find it a deadly piece of evidence.'

It was apparent from their expressions that the battle of nerves was won.

'How much do you want?'

'I think one-third would be a fair share, don't you? But I'm not greedy. Make it to the nearest thousand. I'll settle for three thousand pounds.'

'The money's not here.'

'I didn't imagine it would be. But I can wait. Or rather, I'll come back in one hour's time. OK?'

Purling nodded.

'Fine. Meanwhile, of course, I'll keep this memento of Miss Bishop's splendid performance yesterday.' He put the plastic envelope containing the hair back in his pocket.

An hour later, he returned to the house. The money was on the table in a large envelope. It was in bundles of £5 notes which he flicked through.

'I won't stop to count it now,' he said genially. 'It looks about right. I trust you not to have cheated me.'

He reached into his pocket and pulled out the plastic envelope.

'And now I'll keep my side of the bargain,' he said, at the same moment extracting his cigarette lighter and putting a flame to the envelope.

He gave a little puff to blow the wispy ashes in their direction and then, before they could react, quickly left the room.

Once home, he carefully counted the money. There was exactly £3000. It made him positively purr with pleasure. A situation had been retrieved and turned to triumphant account. How fortunate the evening paper had described the colour of Miss Bishop's hair! And what a splendid piece of bluff it had been to get them to believe he really had picked up one of her hairs off the bank floor! It showed what a poor state their nerves were in! They could have learnt something from him before embarking on criminal enterprises. . . .

And now F. Barr really was ready to be finally buried. He'd had a short but highly profitable life, but henceforward he'd be no more than a memory locked away in his creator's mind.

It was about a week later that Terry happened to see a short paragraph tucked away on an inner page of a newspaper. It read: 'Rodney Purling aged 25 and Candy Bishop aged 23 appeared at Greenwich Magistrates Court yesterday charged with stealing £10,000 from the City and Provincial Bank. They were remanded in custody for one week.'

At lunchtime that day he bought all the newspapers he could find, but with little satisfaction. Only two of them carried the story and neither of these disclosed what had led to their being arrested and charged. The bare mention, however, was enough to give him food for thought.

His plan had been to remain in his present job for a couple of months or so and then to hand in his notice. Exactly what he would do after that he hadn't yet decided. Meanwhile the best part of £5000 lay secure in a safe deposit, awaiting his whim.

After viewing the new development from every possible angle he reached the conclusion that he had no need to worry, as even if Purling and his girl did open their mouths to the police his tracks were well enough covered to thwart any search. Though obviously a full-scale police inquiry into F. Barr's activities must by now be under way, not that any reference to it had appeared in the newspapers.

Such was his confidence that it wasn't long before he was congratulating himself on the smart bit of opportunism which had relieved Purling and the girl of £3000 before the law stepped in and presumably relieved them of the rest. He couldn't help smiling as he contemplated it.

As the weeks went by without so much as a small ripple to disturb his peace of mind, he almost forgot about Purling and Candy Bishop. Indeed there was nothing to remind him of them.

And then one morning in the very week he was proposing to hand in his resignation, the intercom on his desk buzzed and Mr Bisgood's clear and always slightly testy voice came through.

'Come along to my room a moment, Mears.'

Puzzled, but with no sense of apprehension, he got up from his desk, straightened his tie and took the lift down two floors to the corridor where the partners had their offices. A quiet knock and he turned the handle to enter. Mr Bisgood was sitting at his desk and in his visitor's chair was a rather pleasant looking man in his early thirties, neatly dressed and obviously quite at ease.

'This is Detective Sergeant James,' Mr Bisgood said without ceremony. 'He wants to ask you some questions.'

For a second Terry felt as if a bucket of icy water had been flung in his face, though he prayed that his expression gave nothing away.

'Of course,' he said when he dared to use his voice.

Sergeant James gave an approving nod and glanced at Mr Bisgood who was staring at Terry as though he had sprouted a second set of ears.

'Mr Bisgood has suggested we could go into the office next door which, I gather, is unoccupied this morning,' Sergeant James said and got up.

'Yes, you won't be disturbed there,' Mr Bisgood said grimly.

Terry followed the officer out and into the other room. As soon as they were seated, Sergeant James said agreeably:

'I expect you can guess what it's all about?'

'I'm afraid not. I've no idea. I imagine it's something arising in my work.'

Sergeant James shook his head as though he felt let down by Terry's answer. 'No, it's nothing to do with your work. It's to do with cheques.' Terry felt his face muscles go suddenly stiff. 'I can see you know what I'm talking about.'

He managed to shake his head. 'Cheques,' he muttered. 'I've no idea what you're talking about.'

'Come off it, Mr Barr.'

'Barr? I don't know who you mean. My name's Mears.'

'Do you deny that you worked an ingenious cheque fraud in the name of Barr?'

'I most certainly do. I've never heard of anyone named Barr.'

Sergeant James reached for a pen and then passed it across to Terry with a blank sheet of paper. 'Would you mind writing F. Barr on that piece of paper?'

'Why should I?'

'Frightened to do so?'

'Not a bit if it'll please you.'

'Yes, it'll please me.'

Three quarters of an hour later, Sergeant James realised he was not going to break his quarry down. He got up. 'I'd like you to accompany me to your digs.'

'Why?'

'I'd like to have a look round.'

'Supposing I refuse?'

'I'll soon get a search warrant.'

Terry shrugged. 'All right, then.'

Sergeant James' search was thorough and his disappointment became more and more obvious when he failed to find anything. All the while, Terry watched him impassively.

At the end, James said, 'I'll be wanting to see you again. Not thinking of leaving this address, are you?'

'No.'

'I take it you'd have no objection to standing on an identification parade, would you?'

Terry swallowed uncomfortably. 'What if I do?'

'I'll have to arrange for various witnesses to get a glimpse of you under conditions less fair to yourself. It's up to you.'

'OK, I'll attend your identification parade.'

'Right, I'll fix one up. Probably tomorrow.'

Terry went back to work in the afternoon, but found himself quite unable to concentrate. He suddenly had the feeling that everyone around him was a police spy.

The next morning the officer phoned to say that the parade was fixed up and that he would call for Terry in a car at noon.

They drove to a police station where Sergeant James

led the way to a large room in the basement where eleven other young men of near enough Terry's age and build were hanging around.

A uniformed inspector took charge, formed them into a line and told Terry that he could position himself wherever he chose and moreover that he could change his place in the line after each witness.

The first witness was a young man whom Terry vaguely remembered as being one of the bank tellers on the first day of operations. Terry held his breath as the young man passed him. He reached the end of the line.

'I'm afraid it's no good, it's so long ago ...' he murmured before being ushered out.

The next witness was as negative, but the one after pointed at the man standing three away from Terry.

'That's like him, I think,' he said uncertainly, 'but I can't be sure.'

After two more had been introduced to the parade and had failed to pick anyone out, Terry began to relax. After all, it wasn't surprising that they were unable, months after the event, to identify someone whom they'd seen for only a minute or so and whose features they'd had no reason at the time to try and remember.

Obviously the police didn't have enough against him to justify a charge without an identification or they would have done so. He had the impression that they had got on to him through a sheer slogging routine check by the bank of customers' records. They had found some similarity in the writing of T. Mears and F. Barr to warrant further probing by the police. ...

Terry surreptitiously crossed his fingers. His luck was holding. He heard the door open and close again and waited for the next witness to pass across his line of vision. ...

'This is the man. I'd recognise him anywhere.'

For a second, Terry stood too numbed to realise what had happened, as he stared stupidly into the face of Rodney Purling.

Detective Sergeant James was in high good humour sitting in the back of the car with Terry as they were driven to Greenwich where Terry was to be charged. He chattered away and seemed quite unconcerned by his companion's dejected silence.

'I must say it was a neat little scheme you had, though you did rather push your luck, you know. What was it, thirty banks a day you visited? Things being how they are these days, you were almost bound to clash with someone else's bit of activity in such a busy nip around. The law of averages was against you. Nevertheless, you nearly got away with it.' He chuckled. 'Funny that that chap Purling was the only one able to pick you out!'

NOTE: *Since this story was written, banks have intro-duced measures to prevent themselves being de-frauded in this manner.*

INCIDENT IN TROLETTA

by John Wainwright

The summer breeze raced across the Ionian Sea. It stroked the waves in the Gulf of Taranto, sped inland over Basilicata, beyond Metaponto and into the village of Troletta. It stirred the dust around the hem of Father Ghiberti's robe.

The priest felt the breeze and offered a quick, silent prayer of thanks. The crops – the wheat, the maize, the vines, the olives – needed rain. Without rain, the normal paucity of the village would turn to poverty. The villagers needed the crops, and the crops needed rain, and the breeze was a herald of rain to come. Therefore, the priest gave thanks for the breeze.

He turned a corner, and a frown etched lines across his face as he saw the jeep standing by the door of his church.

It was an old jeep, and the only jeep in Troletta. It was a battered war-veteran, and should have been consigned to some motor-car's knacker-yard years ago. It had been brought by the American Army, and had changed hands a dozen times before being commandeered by Lieutenant Borroto, the local Chief of Police.

Borroto was with the jeep.

As Father Ghiberti approached, Borroto hoisted his bulk from the driver's seat. His khaki shirt had smudges of damp under the arms and around the waist, and his pumpkin face shone with sweat.

'Good-day to you, Father.'

Borroto's voice was curiously high-spirited. Especially for such a gross man. The combination was reminiscent of eunuchised harem guards.

He grinned and added: 'The weather does not improve. I think we are having a foretaste of your hell.'

Ghiberti said: 'Do not scoff at eternal damnation, Lieutenant Borroto,' and the words were a reprimand. He disliked this great ox of a man with the squeaky voice and the arrogant ways.

Borroto's grin broadened. He removed his peaked cap, mopped his sweat-soaked hair with a large, white handkerchief. He replaced the cap and stuffed the handkerchief back into its pocket before he spoke again.

'Louis Parrino is dead.'

It was a casual statement. It carried less emotion than when Borroto had remarked upon the weather.

'God rest his soul.' Ghiberti crossed himself, then shrugged and added: 'It was to be expected. He was a libertine. Too old for such ways. I warned him. His heart could not stand such strain. To behave as he behaved ...'

'Not his heart. His throat.'

The priest did not immediately understand.

Borroto said: 'Somebody used a knife.'

'Somebody has killed him?'

The priest looked startled and, for the first time, showed interest.

'Somebody has killed him,' agreed Borroto. 'It was a thorough job. He was almost decapitated. There was great butchery – a needless cutting.'

The Police Chief shook his head in mocking disapproval of such unnecessary violence.

Ghiberti said: 'You have arrested the murderer?'

'No.'

'But you know?'

'We will find him.'

'Him?'

'Soon.'

'You already know the murderer is a man?'

'Of course.'

The priest hesitated, then said: 'The knife ... it is a woman's weapon.'

'They say such things.'

'And they are not so?'

Borroto chuckled. It was a phlegmy, tittering sound. An animal noise. A repulsive noise.

'Father, you do not know women. The weapon is a woman's ... but not the target. The belly, or the back. *That* is where a woman uses a knife. She sticks. She does not cut.'

'You have given thought to such things.'

The remark was as near to a sneer as the priest would permit himself.

'Of course. It is my profession.'

Ghiberti sighed. The egotism of the Police Chief was proof against criticism, and the mild sarcasm had bounced off the hard shell of his self-importance.

Ghiberti said: 'We are a village of almost a thousand souls. Half of them are men.'

Borroto raised a quizzical eyebrow.

'You have a great problem, Lieutenant Borroto.'

'The murderer is of this village,' said Borroto.

'It would seem so. We are isolated, and I have heard of no strangers.'

Borroto's tiny eyes gleamed. His smile was a compound of satisfaction and anticipation.

He said: 'You are right, Father. He is of this village, and we will find him ... you and I.'

'I am a priest, not a policeman.' Ghiberti's tone carried a reprimand. 'I save souls. I leave the tracking down of men to those of your ... "profession".'

Lieutenant Borroto shook his head, slowly, then spoke as if explaining some fundamental truth to a backward child.

He said: 'Father, the man has committed a great sin.'

'A very great sin,' agreed the priest.

'He will wish to rid himself of its burden.'

'If he is a good Christian.'

'Be sure he is a good Christian, Father.' Borroto chuckled, again. 'Only the most righteous anger – the most *Christian* of angers – could drive a man to so much savagery.'

The priest said: 'Your cynicism sickens me, Lieutenant Borroto,' and the unaccustomed edge to his voice gave evidence of the state of his temper.

'I am no cynic, Father Ghiberti.' Borroto shrugged and spread out his palms. 'I deal in facts. If the facts are unsavoury, they are none the less true. It is a fact that Louis Parrino was an evil man. That some of his friends may have disliked him. That some may even have wished him dead. But it is also a fact that, had they killed him, it would have been a clean killing. There would have been no wholesale butchery.'

Ghiberti said: 'You distort the truth, Borroto.'

'That would take a stronger man than I.'

'You bend goodness to your own ends.'

'And you,' countered Borroto, 'preach the hatred of all evil.'

'You deal in bad logic, Borroto. There is a killing. There is an excess of savagery. Therefore, you name one of my congregation as the murderer.'

'Of course, Father.'

'Without cause.'

'Forgive me, Father Ghiberti, but with *good* cause.

Consider. Your religion is based upon Goodness. You teach the hatred of all things evil. Therefore, only goodness – only Christian goodness – can hate evil so much.'

For the space of six heart-beats Father Ghiberti looked into the eyes of Lieutenant Borroto. For that length of time the priest allowed his loathing to show itself.

Then he turned and hurried up the steps and into his church.

It was a brooding dawn. The breeze was like a breath from an open oven. Dark, anvil clouds piled high above the Apennine foothills and the rain had already reached Matera. But Troletta remained parched – a calidarium of restless sleepers – as Father Ghiberti walked the deserted streets to his church.

It was cooler inside the church. Shafts of light slanted through the stained glass, sparkling a million dust motes before reflecting themselves against polished wood and brass, and soaking themselves into the eternal tranquillity of grey stonework.

The priest knelt and made his morning prayer.

Then he moved to the Confessional, and a rustling from behind the curtain gave evidence of an early penitent.

A voice said: 'Are you there, Father?'

It was a man's voice. Quietly respectful. Untroubled, and without tremor.

'I am here.'

'Father ... I have killed Louis Parrino.'

After the slight pause, the admission was made without hesitation.

A sudden surge of anger clouded the priest's brain. In the dark corners of his mind he heard the mocking echoes of Borroto's chuckle and the words '... only goodness – only Christian goodness – can hate evil so much'.

He went a little mad, and centuries-old disciplines were forgotten or ignored.

His voice was brittle when he said : 'Who are you?'

'Antonio Piretti.'

The anonymity of the Confessional was destroyed, without reluctance and without question.

The silence stretched itself into half a minute of eternity. Then the priest spoke again.

'Go to the side chapel.'

'Father?'

'Leave me. I will join you when I have reached a decision.'

Antonio Piretti.

There are men of whom the word 'stature' means more than mere physique. Antonio Piretti was such a man. His five-foot-six-inch frame was thin to emacia-tion; a thing of bone and whipcord encased in wrinkled parchment. His chocolate-brown eyes, set deep in the folds and lines of his face, had a pride born of simple honesty. His clothes – threadbare shirt and frayed trousers – were bleached from overwashing, and worn with humble regality.

It seemed right that such a man should stand above Father Ghiberti as the priest sat, hunched and silent, clenching white-knuckled hands between his knees.

'Father, I seek forgiveness.'

It was not a demand – the tone was too respectful. It was a reminder of the reason for his presence.

The priest raised his head, and said : 'Why did you do it?' and his voice was a plea; a cry for some straw of sanity to which he could cling.

'It was necessary.'

'No.'

'Believe me, Father.'

'To kill a man is *never* necessary.'

'It was necessary, Father,' insisted Piretti.

The priest sighed, then said: 'Why was it necessary?'

'He had lived too long.'

'That is no answer.'

'He had committed too much wickedness.'

'Who are you, to judge?'

'He stole my land,' said Piretti, in a flat, emotionless voice. 'The lawyers said he had the right. They said the law was his. But, he stole my land. Because of this, I became poor. My wife died. She would not have died, had I not been poor. Had it not been for Louis Parrino.'

'I know all this.'

'Then you know my heart was filled with hatred. But you spoke to me, and I prayed, and the hatred left me. I learned to forgive. Even Louis Parrino.'

'Then, why?'

'But not my Margurite!' For the first time Piretti's voice was flecked with passion. 'He should not have done this terrible thing.'

'Margurite?'

'He plays games ... this Louis Parrino. He plays games, with children.'

'I don't know what ...'

'He is an animal. He should have walked on all fours. He was not a man.'

'We judge too harshly. And we are not ...'

'He forced my Margurite to his bed,' rasped Piretti. 'He, and the thugs who dance attendance upon him.'

'Mother of God!'

Father Ghiberti's whispered exclamation of horror

was thrown back by the walls of the side chapel.

'A fifteen-year-old child.' Piretti's voice was tight with fury. 'He was an old man. He had had all the women he wanted. He had stolen all the land he wished to steal. So, he stole the honour of a fifteen-year-old child.'

There was a silence. Hate-heavy. Filled with visions of intemperance and lechery. A silence which was an explanation of a killing.

Antonio Piretti spoke again, and his voice was once more under control.

He said: 'My daughter is with child. It is better that the child is a fatherless bastard than that Louis Parrino can claim to be its parent.'

Father Ghiberti rose to his feet. Twice he made as if to speak, but said nothing.

Then, he said: 'Antonio Piretti, we have long been friends.'

'I have valued your friendship.'

'And I yours.'

'I am glad.'

'But I am a priest. There are things I can never do.'

'You are my confessor.'

'Not in this thing,' said Ghiberti, sadly.

Piretti sighed, then said: 'Are you refusing me absolution, Father?'

'I must . . . you know I must.'

'You are my confessor,' repeated Piretti.

The priest said: 'Absolution comes only with repentance, and you do not repent.'

'I am sorry I killed him.'

'But not sorry that he is dead.'

'There is a difference?'

'There is a difference,' said Ghiberti, sadly.

Piretti sighed, then said: 'I am not sorry that he is

dead. I am glad that he is dead.'

'That, also, is a sin.'

Piretti made no immediate reply. A vague melancholy misted his eyes, and when he spoke again it was with simple, sombre conviction.

He said: 'I will be honest, Father. I will not hide the truth from you. I desired absolution before I left the village.'

'You are leaving?'

'If I stay Lieutenant Borroto will question me. The matter of Margurite can not remain a secret forever. Then Borroto will question me. I would have left the district. Left Italy. Gone to Malta ... perhaps beyond. But, before I go, I must have absolution. And from Father Ghiberti, my friend.'

'You ask the impossible.'

'I would accept any penance.'

Father Ghiberti shook his head. 'You have chosen your own penance. To live with your sin, without regret. I pity you. But I cannot help you.'

Again, there was a silence.

Again, Piretti sighed.

Then he turned and walked from the chapel, into the body of the church and towards the iron-studded door.

Black clouds swarmed and tumbled overhead. Thunder battered the eardrums, like celestial timpani. Lightning streaked and shimmered across the horizon. In the streets of Troletta the first drops of rain spattered themselves into the dust. Each one a globulet of hope. Each one punching its own tiny crater into the thirsty earth.

Father Ghiberti rose from his knees.

He was tired of praying. He felt as if he had been praying for a lifetime. Praying to his God ... praying

to his Holy Mother. Praying for himself – for wisdom –
for guidance – for courage. Praying for Antonio Piretti
– for repentance – for forgiveness. Praying for the tormented soul of Louis Parrino.

All that prayer.

And not a single answer.

He shook his head to clear his mind, turned from the
altar and saw Lieutenant Borroto.

Borroto was grinning. A fixed, Jack-o-Lantern grin.

He said: 'Were you praying for the murderer,
Father?'

The priest did not answer.

'No-matter.' Borroto's lips curled into a sneer. 'Our
friend, Antonio Piretti, has given himself up.'

'Given himself up?'

Borroto nodded.

'To *you*?'

'But, of course. Did I not say we would find him? . . .
you and I?'

Ghiberti said: 'I will have no part of this,' and his
voice was harsh with an anguish he could not fully
understand.

'You had no choice, Father.' Borroto's voice was a
soothing mockery. 'What else could you do? You *had*
to send him to me.'

'I did not send him to you!'

Borroto's laugh was a little like the idiot scream of
a hyena.

'I would not send Satan himself to you, Lieutenant
Borroto.'

'He requests absolution.'

'I cannot give him absolution.'

'He wishes to know whether he may expect you today. Or whether you would prefer to await the more

technically correct time ... immediately before his execution.'

Father Ghiberti ran from the church.

The slanting rods of rain hurled earthwards from the angry sky.

They smashed into the priest's face, and mingled with his tears.